Advance Praise for *Tauhou*

"Brilliantly written in the best of Māori and Coast Salish practices of story, *Tauhou* is teeming with possibility, love, and dreaming otherwise."

— Leanne Betasamosake Simpson, author of
Noopiming: The Cure for White Ladies

"The stories in this collection move like the waves of the ocean that divide Vancouver Island and Aotearoa. Once you emerge from *Tauhou*'s narrative depths, you'll miss its imagination, its rhythms, its heart."

— Alicia Elliott, author of
A Mind Spread Out on the Ground

"Kōtuku Titihuia Nuttall's *Tauhou* is a brilliant example of what language can do when forged with intentional hands and a fantastic mind. Nuttall's work binds words in a way that doesn't hold too tightly but steadfastly contains the many Ancestors present in Nuttall's life and work, weaving together a tapestry of nuance and witnessing. Masterful dialogue and rich scenes move emotions like the currents around Aotearoa and the Salish Seas, a beautiful display of lyricism that loudly proclaims that Kōtuku Titihuia Nuttall belongs in the crescendo of rising voices in CanLit. *Tauhou* is not a collection to miss!"

— jaye simpson, author of
it was never going to be okay

"A work of great significance, integrity, craft, and poise."
— Alison Whittaker, author of *Blakwork*

"Kōtuku Titihuia Nuttall takes threads made from all the colours of the Indigenous experience and crosses them over oceans, cultures, and time."
— Tayi Tibble, author of *Poukahangatus* and *Rangikura*

"*Tauhou* is a search for answers, of finding ways to live with the truth. Some of the stories are like fables, others like poetry, and all are a sheer joy to read. A longing for home resonates, a gift for those of us searching for our island also."
— *Kete Books*

"This one's for the lovers of language, lean prose-poetry you can dip in and out of and think about for hours. Best read beside a large body of water."
— *Woman Magazine*

TAUHOU

A NOVEL

Kōtuku Titihuia Nuttall

ANANSI

Published in New Zealand in 2022 by Te Herenga Waka University Press
Published in Canada and the USA in 2023 by House of Anansi Press Inc.
houseofanansi.com

House of Anansi Press is committed to protecting our natural environment.
This book is made of material from well-managed FSC®-certified forests,
recycled materials, and other controlled sources.

House of Anansi Press is a Global Certified Accessible™ (GCA by Benetech)
publisher. The ebook version of this book meets stringent accessibility
standards and is available to readers with print disabilities.

27 26 25 24 23   1 2 3 4 5

Library and Archives Canada Cataloguing in Publication

Title: Tauhou : a novel / Kōtuku Titihuia Nuttall.
Names: Nuttall, Kōtuku Titihuia, author.
Identifiers: Canadiana (print) 20220431310 | Canadiana (ebook) 20220431337 |
ISBN 9781487011697 (hardcover) | ISBN 9781487011703 (EPUB)
Classification: LCC PR9639.4.N88 T38 2023 | DDC 823/.92—dc23

Cover artwork: Kōtuku Titihuia Nuttall
Text design and typesetting: Alysia Shewchuk

*House of Anansi Press is grateful for the privilege to work on and create
from the Traditional Territory of many Nations, including the Anishinabeg,
the Wendat, and the Haudenosaunee, as well as the Treaty Lands of the
Mississaugas of the Credit.*

Canada Council
for the Arts
Conseil des Arts
du Canada

ONTARIO ARTS COUNCIL
CONSEIL DES ARTS DE L'ONTARIO
an Ontario government agency
un organisme du gouvernement de l'Ontario

With the participation of the Government of Canada
Avec la participation du gouvernement du Canada | Canadä

*We acknowledge for their financial support of our publishing program the
Canada Council for the Arts, the Ontario Arts Council, and the Government
of Canada.*

Printed and bound in Canada

MIX
Paper from
responsible sources
FSC
www.fsc.org
FSC® C016245

While this book has been written with care for its readers and characters alike, it does contend with violent themes that should be approached with caution. These include residential schools, domestic abuse, and mental illness. I've done my best to handle these subjects with respect and to illustrate how Indigenous lives transform and transcend our trauma. That being said, take care when reading.

— Kōtuku Titihuia Nuttall

For Māmā

Tukua mai he kapunga oneone ki ahau hei tangi māku.

Send me a handful of soil so I may grieve over it.

CONTENTS

ĆENQÁLES / HOT EARTH

ĆENKI,LES / EARTH BORN AGAIN

ĆENTOŁEN

COLD EARTH

DAUGHTER

Creator throws them into the ocean, Mother and
Daughter, to become islands. This transformation is
accompanied by a covenant of mutual care between
the people and the new land.

They lie side by side. Mother wraps herself ever so
slightly around Daughter.

An island is a golf green, a private hunting ground
for exotic animals, a scientific reserve. An island
can be bought with money, if you're into that sort of
thing. An island is the only thing between you and
the bottom of the ocean.

SN̲ITȻEŁ

The train cuts through the swampy grasses
quickly — it's barely on time. Behind the huge exotic
conifers, passengers can see the body of the express-
way demanding its feed. Men work round the clock
to cut through the earth and replace what they
remove with concrete. Farther down the road is the
makeshift factory that blows plumes of dust and
fuel into the air. The hills all around grow pines to
be milled. Farther down, the forest becomes quarry.
Kererū swoop from those hills towards the other
island, through the smog.

When they built the concrete factory across the
bay, on the other island, the workers had to create
a small town of shacks and poorly made houses.
Eagles watched as all the waste from the factory
was dumped into the inlet nearby. Those waters had

been the bluest, that land the most full of game. The factory foreman had the biggest house of all, surrounded by new plantings of fruit trees and invasive hedging. The lady of the house loved to garden. Her roses still poke through the overgrown blackberry a hundred years later, when the settlement is no more than concrete foundations in a clearing.

Later, when the people were allowed to hunt there again — on their own sacred land, where the first man fell from the sky as rain and built the first village on earth — deer were killed and carried home to be butchered. It was joyful. Knives were sharpened to cut the animals open, only to find their stomachs lined with concrete dust.

WATER

Cousins

The morning air is still. Hīnau steps out of her apartment and messes around trying to lock it behind her. The mechanism of the lock is loose in all the wrong places. It probably doesn't help that her key is bent out of shape, but she tries to ignore that. She achieves a level of lockedness and hurries down the stairwell towards the street, which is more of a boardwalk. The sea spray reaches up towards Hīnau.

There is water all around, everywhere. The condos and apartment blocks are built out and out and out, until most of them rest atop stilts in the water. More than half of the city sits over the sea now, on metal beams made to sway with waves and tides. The buildings rise up so high they become glassy pillars that reflect the sunlight, which bounces and sparkles off the ocean. The most expensive condos are still clos-est to the shore. Beyond those at the shoreline are the smaller, cheaper, and more poorly built buildings. A small tramline operates between this shore and the floating suburbs farther out into the water, carrying the workers who live on the sea onto the land to work.

The water is dark and still. There isn't any wind but there is cloud, which threatens to turn the ocean. Hīnau steps carefully out from under the awning and onto the perpetually wet concrete, bracing for the chill. The streets are empty. Plenty of the more important office workers don't need to be awake just yet. The most organized will barely be having breakfast now, scrolling through the news and wearing down their molars on tough but nutritious granola. Hīnau doesn't have to get up as early as some of the other workers — those who live farther out into the sea and have longer commutes, with earlier starting hours.

Hīnau tries to avoid puddles of salt water. There are barnacles growing on the lowest rungs of the side-walk, where the sea rises often enough to sustain them. They're closed up now, asleep, waiting for the sea to return and wash them over with feed.

There's no one else at Hīnau's stop. She lives far out from the land with most of the factory workers, even though she has the employment status to live closer to the islands. The tram is a few minutes away, but she feels it start to shake the boardwalk, its bright lights searching ahead, illuminating the wet. The buildings sway very softly as the tram continues its rattling approach.

When they were built, these residential blocks were poured straight into the water in a mould. They rose suddenly from the middle of the ocean and weren't thoroughly quality checked by government officials. They were quick, short-term solutions. All the lands where reserves had been were becoming golf courses and mansions. Whole families were asked to leave their homes and were offered little compensation. Some of the most successful band members were able to invest in buying the land back for themselves and their communities, though the land which was once communal became private. Council leaders and chiefs agreed on a solution for the displaced band members. They would build out onto the ocean, to live as they had once before — on the water, but replacing canoes with high-density housing.

The buildings were made all at once, as if on a factory line. Tenants were moved in straight away, with preference being given to those who worked in the biggest factories and fish farms. Though the commute was long, the housing was stable and new. It was a step up for most, except those in the lower floors — at and below water level. Originally the buildings had trialed submarine living. Complaints of damp and dark, and the ominous dripping, were ignored. One by one, and then all at once, those lower floors had flooded, until every submarine apartment was underwater. Several hundred people died in their own homes, stuck in their living rooms, floating to the ceiling until they drowned, and sinking to the floor. The experiment was put on hold, and the newer buildings were made without those underwater levels. They would be raised up on stilts until they were just above the tidelines.

Hīnau checks her bag and brushes off her clothes. The tram approaches and stops for her. She presents her ticket to the conductor and walks towards one of the empty seats. She's tired and her tooth aches. She suspects she has a cavity. Just the other day she grew a mouth ulcer on the skin and gum closest to the upset tooth. Hīnau wonders if a cavity can spread to flesh. The tram sets off, jostling all the stuff in her bag. Her pens and notes and binders — work she has taken home for the weekend, hoping to make a little extra money. She has a job in the tribal propaganda office for the southeast peninsula of this island. It's a middle-of-the-road job; she has some education, which helped her get the role, but she doesn't earn enough to have any left over after necessities and the occasional night out.

The job requires that she write all kinds of things. Local guide information, educational literature, signs, directions, maps. She writes things for outsiders to stop and read — to learn what these places were like before and where they're headed now.

The heaters on the tram are broken, like they are every winter. Hīnau is wearing her grandmother's dog hair toque, which keeps her head and ears warm, but she's left the zipper of her jacket open. The fabric of her blouse is thin and shimmery. She felt beautiful when she put it on, but now the stagnant carriage air is icy and chilling the skin of her chest. Self-conscious, she readjusts her jacket, doing up the zip to her chin, wincing as she snags it on her neck in the process. The lights of the tram illuminate farther than she can see.

Salal has just made Hīnau a cup of tea as she arrives in the office. Salal's aunt owns a good portion of her family's winter village site. She is still free to harvest as she wishes. The tea is nettle with plenty of honey. Hīnau watches Salal dip her spoon into the pot of honey and twirl and drizzle it over her mug, a glistening ribbon that dissolves upon contact with the hot water.

"Here." Salal hands it to her. "Drink this."

"Kia ora." Hīnau takes a sip, tasting the earthy nettle underneath the honey.

"How was the ride in?"

"Same. Fine. How about you?"

"Cold. Nice. I walked through the park."

They hold their tea quietly for a moment. The building's radiators hum and clang. Salal has been diffusing something in the office, tea tree or mānuka maybe.

"Are you going out tonight?"

"If we finish the harbour signs," says Salal, "I might treat myself."

"Have I missed the announcements?"

"No, you weren't that late, really. I saw Yarrow down the hall a moment ago. I'm sure they'll call us in soon."

The office starts the morning with prayers and announcements in different languages — Hul̓q̓umín̓um̓ first and then the foremost dialect of te reo Māori.

The phone rings. It takes calls only from inside the building. Salal moves to pick it up and starts a conversation with whoever is on the other end.

Hīnau settles into her desk, unpacking her things. She has a computer and a phone. The desk is recycled timber. Salal's uncle worked on the commission for these departmentally issued desks, which used wood that wasn't good enough for carvers — offcuts mostly. No part of the tree went to waste, Salal said. The gardens inside and out used the cedar shavings as mulch so they wouldn't be left to blend into the mud of a carver's yard.

Hīnau opens her emails and drinks her tea. The honey irritates her sore tooth, yet she hopes the nettle will do something for the rest of her body. There are new messages, but she's only been copied into them. It's important they get read, but she doesn't have to reply. Above her desk a lamp mimics sunlight — the office lights produce the full spectrum of colours needed to feed plants effectively. The office designers had been trying to achieve the feeling of being outdoors, but the overwhelming effect is one of displacement. What would one be doing at a desk outside?

Salal says, "All right," and drops the phone back onto its base before taking a seat behind Hīnau. She grimaces and points upwards. "That was the chief's office. They're not happy with the draft texts we sent them."

"Ah. Well, I guess we know what we're doing today."

Salal sips her tea and raises her eyebrows over the cup. "Sure do."

Then Yarrow sticks her head in on the way to the meeting room. She tells them to hurry up and follow her.

They wait for her to leave and sit for a moment, finishing their tea before making a move towards the meeting room.

Hīnau likes sharing an office with Salal. They're cousins, though they aren't sure how yet. But Salal treats Hīnau as if they're sisters anyway. Their fathers sound like similar men, so badly hurt they couldn't help but pain the others around them too. But it's decades later and they're not here anymore and Hīnau and Salāl care about one another. Even when the mahi gets stressful, they still act with kindness and respect.

Hīnau is looking back over all their work from the last few weeks, months even. She knows it will all be taken apart and reconstituted into consumable information by copywriters — and will be full of cultural or historical fallacies and hypocrisies. She still gets irritated by this, but the chief's office will sign it off later and let them move on, which is all anyone really needs.

"What do you think about all this?" Hīnau highlights parts of the initial drafts pertaining to the old houses that were on the cultural blocks of land. It is made up of testimony from elders and knowledge keepers who used to live there, even before this relocation. There were still some buildings from before the land was separated off into reserves a few hundred years ago.

"I thought it was good, but overall it's too archaic. They'll want something a bit more about the current developments," Salal says.

"Which you know more about than me — do you want to take care of that, then?"

"Yeah, all right. Send me the most recent version you've been working on."

Hīnau is glad to hand off the work — they're both

stressed, and when the day is done, both agree emphat-
ically to an after-work drink.

The bar they visit most often is near the office. Hīnau
and Salal arrive straight from work and order drinks.
The bartender starts muddling aromatics and pungent
herbs, adding ice and clear liquor, and slides the glasses
towards the women. Salal takes a particularly large
gulp before opening her purse on the bar.

"Hīnau. I didn't want to do this at the office, but I
have something to show you."

"Okay." Hīnau scratches her fingernails against the
heavy base of her glass. "Shoot."

"I found this photo at my aunt's house. I'm not sure
how useful it will be. Either way, it felt important to
show you, at least."

Salal opens a small envelope and pulls out an old
photo. It is barely in colour, halfway between black and
white and the dull sepia primaries of photos from the
eighties. Hīnau takes it by the edges. In the centre of
the photo are two men and an old woman. The photo
is cheesily posed. It looks like it could possibly be
Christmas, or maybe a birthday. Hīnau looks closely
at all their faces. They look familiar to her, especially
the man on the right—a man she's seen only once or
twice before. He is younger in the photo than she's

ever seen him and smiling a genuine kind of smile.

"That's my dad," Hīnau says.

"I thought it might be." Salal looks like she might cry.

"Who are the other people?"

"That's my dad and his mother. That's our grandmother."

Hīnau feels her heart stop. She tries to look closer.

"I knew we were close family — I assumed — I wanted us to be — " Salal stops for a moment. "But no one would tell me anything, and you didn't know his full name, so I had to guess a little."

"I can't believe I'm holding this photo."

"It's yours, if you want it. We have copies."

"Are you sure?"

"Of course, we'll get you more. Aunty has other albums you might be interested in."

"Yes! Please!" Hīnau wants to scream and yell. She settles for jiggling in her seat, rocking up and down.

"Now, we better set up a time to go visit the village — we have to take you home!"

They finish their drinks, stuck between crying and laughing. Then Salal makes a plan on a bar napkin: a day and a time and a map. They have a few more drinks together, the cousins, before going their separate ways home, Salal walking farther into the land, and Hīnau catching her tram back out over the water.

The Village

They have to drive to get there. The village is set quite a ways from the tramline, which doesn't even run all the way inland. Salal drives her mother's old Jeep, full of fishing gear and gardening equipment. The ocean glistens and fades away as they take the aging highway inland. Salal sings along to the radio, which cuts in and out beneath the wind whipping through their open windows. Hīnau rests her head on her hand and watches the trees thicken and green up.

It takes an hour or so to reach a tall chain-link fence covered in warning signs. They're written in Hul̓q̓umín̓um̓ and tell visitors to inquire at the band office about visits or to get in touch with the landowners. Salal has keys for all the padlocks and opens the gate, locking it again behind them. The road becomes trail and starts to wind through the trees. Hīnau glimpses a big new house off to the side — a modern cabin: half-glass, half-wood — hiding between the tallest trees. Salal whistles out her window and laughs when she gets a whistle back.

"Aunty Cedar," she says.

They continue a little farther, until Salal hits the brakes and kills the engine.

"We're here!"

It's a dead end in the middle of the dark forest.

"Come on. Grab your stuff." Salal hops out and begins pulling out their day bags. She takes a swig from a waterskin and offers some to Hīnau, who shakes her head.

"Suit yourself. Let's get moving. Aunty's house is just back there. The village is straight through these trees."

Between redwoods and ferns is a thin dirt track. They start off.

"Thanks for bringing me," Hīnau says, trying to tread lightly on the moss at her feet.

"I'm grateful you came. I know it's a little late and probably quite emotional, but this is your home too. Happy homecoming."

Hīnau was born on the other island, the one to the south. It was a quarter of a century ago, when the cities were only just beginning to encroach on the ocean. Her mother lived in a small city in the middle of the island, a student town where she could bike to the university campus. She continued her classes while pregnant. After Hīnau was born, she fixed a baby seat to the back of the bike. In the mornings they would make their way to the campus, down the esplanade with its fluffy pink blossoms. The river meandered slowly beneath the bridge. On the hills to the east, windmills were fixed to the earth like great white dandelion seeds.

Hīnau's father had been hidden away in moving boxes, in notebooks and diaries pasted with evidence of her mother's travels. In summertime, when mother and daughter made their way down south for the holidays, Hīnau could see the other island resting on the horizon. The highway ran all the way down the island, and for at least an hour there was uninterrupted coastline, until they reached the bay where her mother was born. Every summer was the same: unpack the car and greet their cousins. Hīnau's grandmother, Mahuika, would be in the wharekai, slicing grapes for ambrosia. Mahuika's husband would be out in the sun, turning acid red while having a beer with Mahuika's brothers. When Hīnau would turn to catch a final glimpse of the other island, it would be blocked out by the hills that tumbled into the ocean.

Salal walks quickly but doesn't hesitate to stop and show Hīnau things. The huge banana slugs making their way across the leaf litter on the ground, the secret berry patches come summertime. Under the shelter of the trees the air is warm and wet. Behind their trunks the air starts shining blue.

"We're close. That's the lake." Salal raises her arm to touch the space beyond the trees.

It's surprising how quickly the trees open up to the

water. The lake is huge, and Hīnau can barely see the other end. Across the water is a clearing. She sees the toppled wood, the meadow, the figures fixed to the welcome poles.

They make their way round the edge of the lake, where stone has been washed down to sand. Salal has already taken her shoes off, and Hīnau follows suit, the cold water rushing towards her feet. The grasses are green and fresh with the spring thaw. They follow meadow flowers, which are on their way up through the earth, until they're on the other side of the water. Beneath the tall grass, wooden forms lie on the ground, smooth cedar poles blanched by the sun and air.

A long time ago someone took a sharp chisel to the wood and wore it down to this smoothness, creating perfect ringlets of cedar shavings. Hīnau looks at the figures, their faces pressed against the ground; eyes and mouths pull back, but all she sees are cheeks and the tops of their hats, the rounded shapes of their shoulders.

"This is the big house. It used to be painted. Those were fixed to the front." Salal looks over everything carefully. "Only a few decades ago, we would have been stuck here, in the old reserve behind this spot. We would have grown up here together."

"Do you think that would have been a good thing?"

"Probably not, but we might have been less lonely."

Salal takes Hīnau's hand and leads her into the house. "Come on."

The roof is half gone. Above is the brilliant blue of the sky, the edges of the mountains that are still barely tipped with snow. The grass grows to thigh height, even with the lower levels of light. The interior edges of the door are guarded by ancestor figures.

"It's bigger than I thought it would be," Hīnau says. The room is deep and long; hundreds of people could fit inside it easily. She hears the crackling of fires, chatter, laughter. Smoke billows up through the roof. The grass becomes translucent and fades in and out of static.

"Bigger than other longhouses, for sure. I've seen photos of the ones where you grew up. Everyone used to live in here at once."

There are small wooden partitions. Mats appear on the ground, which becomes smooth and hard. People start springing up from mist: a woman with a spindle, spinning animal hair into wool. Hīnau watches them, then looks towards Salal, who isn't reacting at all. They both witness what happens inside the big house. Children appear and chase dogs. Drums and drummers grow out of the mist; the timbre of drumstick on animal skin is watery and thin, water hitting water.

"What does it make you feel, being here?" Hīnau asks.

"I feel like I'm missing out on something," says Salal.

"I feel sad... We're lucky to be here at all. I think about my grandmother. I feel regretful she isn't here to come home." Salal is watching the people laugh and talk and sing together. "Does it feel like home to you?"

Hīnau thinks about this. In some ways it's so alien and unfamiliar. She feels the darkness that hangs off this island, off the people here. It's back home with her mother too, in different ways though, and in smaller quantities.

"It does," Hīnau says. "More than I expected. But it also feels a little like a betrayal." She thinks of the way her mother turns her body away when Hīnau talks about her new home. She thinks about the things her father wrote in the letters that enthralled her mother so much as a teenager. "I'm glad you're here with me, at least."

Salal wraps her arm round Hīnau. In front of them the water is dissipating into mist and rising away through the roof. It grows quiet and cold.

"Do you want to visit the reserve? While we're here anyway. Then we can go visit Aunty for lunch."

"Yes, while we're here, I guess."

Salal guides her back out the door, where the sun hits their faces. There's still a cool breeze, but the light is warm and happy.

"The reserve is this way — forward again."

They carry on, back into the forest.

SX̱IMÁȽEȽ

The ocean is the same every morning, made of the same damp saltwater bay smell. The bridge is ugly-cheap-modern concrete and metal. Below it, harbour seals look up at us. They smile, their rounded grey bellies keeping them afloat in the dirty water. We walk across the bridge to get to the elementary school. The halls are empty, but we cannot remember if it is a holiday or if everyone is in class. Our father will not let us go to school. Usually we enter school grounds to play on the playgrounds only when they're empty.

The women working in the foyer let us stay to look at the fish tank inside, which is a representation of local endemic saltwater ecosystems. It's full of grey-brown stone and sand. Molluscs and invertebrates make their way across the bottom. In the water above, small and skittish fish dart up and down, from each small apartment of rock crannies to the next. Then we leave again through the glass doors. Across the bay is the building we are living in now. It's tall and just as dirty-ugly as the bridge we crossed on our way here.

We walk down the hill to the side, through more residential streets. Brambles of Himalayan blackberry stand between us and the gorge. In the days to come we'll return and pick the fat, black berries into plastic containers. Our mothers will dress us in long and thick protective clothing and let us loose into the thorns and vines. No matter what, the plants will sting and scratch us, leaving our skin cut and irritated for hours afterwards.

Our walk continues through the rows of condos and construction sites towards home. We live several floors up. We are separated by our mothers and spread throughout the different floors of the hotel. Our room is beige and nondescript. My mother buys a small yellow primrose to sit on the table. She sets it on a white china saucer in its black plastic pot.

Then it's just us, the empty room, and the plant.

THE STORY I WON'T WRITE

She sits down to write the story over and over again. She calls it "The Fire" and is enamoured with the implications of this event on her own history. It feels validating to have an external force to directly attribute her unqualified trauma to.

The death certificate rests on her desktop, next to a few applications for postgraduate study and newfound photos of relatives she's never met. There's a sickening swell that accompanies opening it. Any time she looks at the certificate, the blood leaves her head and forces her to lie down. She shouts and cries at her husband or stares out the window until darkness falls. She opens the file regularly anyway, often finding herself double-clicking on the desktop icon before she realizes what she's doing.

She tries to start the story in a dozen different places, with different levels of intimacy. A close and intimate third person, beside her grandmother. Or from a distance: factual, anthropological. She considers the threads she wants to weave in, the statistics, the other stories, the other fires — the ones set at the school over and over again.

But all of these threads require research that hurts her. She can't look at the photos of the children anymore, even when they're pretending to be happy. She can't read the scientific journals documenting suicidal burn victims. Why do they always include photos? She doesn't have the stomach of a doctor or a scientist.

It's romantic to have a reason why. She is obsessed with weaving this tragedy into explanation.

Her grandmother's husband had lit himself on fire during an argument.

It's one of the stories that built her father. She doesn't know how much weight he places on this story himself, and she doesn't care to ask. He talked about it to her mother sometimes. She remembers the shiny flesh of the swirling scars on his chest, which were supposed to be from a sporting accident. It's just something else for her to question or save for a story.

The sand had torn his skin off, though the scar looked like a burn. Like fire had consumed the fat in his flesh and bubbled it away.

Schools burn down all the time, especially Catholic schools, especially residential schools. The one her grandmother attended burned down three times while it was open. Each time it was rebuilt into increasingly evil-looking buildings on the scorched earth. The last fire took place just after her grandmother left the school — just before she had her first child.

They fought all the time; they drank all the time. They had plenty of children and problems and hurts. That afternoon they'd been arguing, and he followed through on the threats he made constantly.

He poured lighter fluid all over himself and struck a match.

The linoleum in the kitchen had to be pulled out and replaced afterwards; the fire dropped onto it and melted holes straight through.

The fire started at his wet fingertips and spread up his arms in one hungry movement.

She tries to start over and over, the first lines.

He had been mistaken.

He hadn't thought he would die.

It wouldn't be the worst thing her grandmother had seen in her life.

He had been mistaken.

SOME THINGS I AM AFRAID OF I

The kids play in the backyard unsupervised. The lawn surrounds a big and ugly dead tree, caught halfway on its journey to stump. It's still tall enough to climb and has a sharpened tip, as if it guards the perimeter of a pā.

The older girl falls off one day and hits the ground so hard she can't breathe. Salal's sisters flock to her, but she ignores them, making for the back door. The other girls disperse again into the yard. She runs towards the house, crying silently for her mother. The woman steps out onto the porch and sees her.

What's wrong?

The girl points and gasps.

You're just winded. It will be over soon.

The woman heads back inside.

Then everyone is gone, and the girl still can't breathe.

SOME THINGS I AM AFRAID OF II

He locks her in the bedroom after the baby is born.
They have all left the snow behind, but the woman
must remain in wintry isolation. The older girl can
visit sometimes, listen to her mother teach the new
baby words. Baby's first word isn't *Mama* or *Pa*, it's
bubble.

Downstairs, Salal must sit amongst her sisters and
their mothers at the dinner table.

Upstairs, the woman celebrates her baby alone.

MOKO

The beat of a tattoo needle is like the steady pounding of a drum. Miro loves it. Any time she doesn't quite feel like herself anymore, she books an appointment with one of her local artists. Seth tattoos in the top of a financial building in the centre of town. She picks something from his flash, or occasionally sends him references from her art history classes. She feels nervous for days before, but once she's in the waiting room, smelling the disinfectant, she gets calm and still. Seth sets up the gun, looping wires through the machine, wrapped in plastic sleeves, like body bags for cords. Parts of it have to be screwed together. Everything is disinfected over and over, and Seth's ungloved hand never touches anything.

Miro settles in. She's getting her back done this time, so she is seated backwards on a chair, resting her forehead against the black massage table. Seth pours ink into little cups. He uses only black now, for health reasons, he says. Some people say that colours are more carcinogenic, that they turn into cancer faster. He dips the gun into one of the small plastic thimbles of ink and buzzes it once, twice, then leaves it on. The monotonous hum will continue for hours. It's just a buzz, but there's a foreboding edge to the sound. A dread. Miro tries to relax her shoulders and pull her back straight down.

Seth asks her about her partner, and Miro asks about his, but they've just broken up and no one has told her yet. She says sorry and shuts up. Seth starts working. The first few drags are awful. Miro immediately regrets her choice of placement. The design is situated between her shoulder blades, below the nape of her neck. The needle is a hot, tearing sensation. A rending. She remembers how harsh tattoos are, the way they send her whole body into shock. She waits for the adrenalin to come. When it does, it arrives in slow waves. Seth is packing the black into her back. It feels like a punch, a blister burning and stinging. She tries to relax. She doesn't want to ruin the good work Seth has started. Miro hopes she's at the end, even at the beginning. She's just waiting for it to be over. She is sitting for hours and hours. Seth is kind and considerate but doesn't talk much as he works. He concentrates hard on his line work, something he's very well-known for.

There's a violence to the gun. The violence necessitates a release. Miro never forgets this. She craves it — until it happens, and then she's waiting for it to stop. Through the windows the hills roll on; the river crawls through the city centre. Seth applies a solid pressure to Miro's shoulders, pushing her down against the bed she's leaning on. It's the firmest platonic touch she's felt in a long time. Sometimes, when she thinks about being alone, she worries she might never be touched again. But for a few hundred dollars an hour, Seth will be there, holding her down as he blackens the layers of dermis underneath her skin.

They take smoke breaks every hour or so and stand around on the rooftop. Miro itches and burns but drinks her Coca-Cola and tries not to think about any of it. Soon Seth is just tidying up, pricking the edges and patches of skin where the ink hasn't taken so well. Then he's done. He takes a photo and thanks Miro for coming in. Miro asks him how much she owes him, and he says a number. She pulls out the cash she got from the ATM before she arrived. He takes it without counting and starts rolling a cigarette. Miro also gives him a cutting of one of her tropical house plants as a tip, a small hoya her housemate grows. When it blooms it will have small waxy flowers that smell like lemon, citrus, faint vanilla. Seth takes it appraisingly. Then Miro is back out on the street, the wind whipping her weeping flesh. The ink will bleed out onto her sheets and clothes for days.

It's easy for Hīnau to find the right kind of tattoo artist. Since she left school and moved islands, old world styles of tattooing have made a comeback. Artists are everywhere and advertising constantly. Without any effort, Hīnau finds herself admiring their handiwork on her friends and co-workers. Hīnau and Salal often go for a drink after work. It never takes long, a beer or two perhaps, for everyone to start talking about all the different kinds of art they have on them: bone carvings, beaded leatherwork, cedar earrings, silver carved into formline totems. Men with handsome graphic thunderbird tattoos, or orcas and bears and eagles. But Hīnau is most excited by the women's tattoos. They are all completed by hand, without the use of a tattoo gun. Plenty of her friends have parallel skin stitch lines down the chin and across the cheeks, or sometimes arrow shapes stretching down from their foreheads into a point that almost touches the space between their eyebrows. Some of her friends wear tattoos like bracelets or anklets. Salal points out differences between regions and tribes to Hīnau.

For their people, it was mostly women who were tattooed. Men would often get markings as reminders of important spiritual journeys or memorable and magical events, but when women came of age, they would receive marks on their faces and hands and feet. When Hīnau takes her friends' hands in hers and examines the lines, they're uneven. The artists have attempted symmetry, but the end result has a comfortingly natural and organic quality. The lines follow the shape of the bodies they adorn, making space for joints, sitting in tandem with the bones that run underneath the skin. Hīnau is enchanted and sometimes jealous.

One time when she's out with her friends, Hīnau finally asks someone for their tattooist's details. They're happy to scribble a name and email address and an @ on a napkin. Without thinking about it too hard, Hīnau resolves to send them a message. Camas, the tattooist, is from up north somewhere, with a slightly different art style and culture to hers. If it were several hundred years ago, her family and Hīnau's would be at war or raiding one another. But such things don't matter anymore, not really. It is joyful to be sharing and reviving each other's ancestors. Excited, Hīnau types her message once she's home and presses send before she can second-guess herself.

Camas lives off of the main highway, down a dirt driveway. Her house is haphazardly maintained, a patchwork of old wood and corrugated iron pinned up against the original walls. In the front of the cabin is a small section of cottage flowers that grow through the fence. There are raised beds of vegetables and flowers to attract bees, mostly borage and calendula. Some nasturtiums make their way through the over-grown gardens, with bright faces of scarlet, mandarin, limoncello.

Hīnau arrives by herself. Salal offered to join her, but Hīnau felt like she should come alone, this time at least. She doesn't mind this now, but she does wish she could have at least seen her mother beforehand. Hīnau makes her way through the humming garden, past the broken-down cars under the awning, covered over by bright-blue tarps. She knocks on the door, which is bordered by slits of sea-green stained glass. A woman answers, wiry, with hennaed hair.

"Hello! Hīnau! Come in, come in." Camas pulls her inside.

"Thank you. Sorry, one minute." Hīnau pushes down on the heel of her shoe to slip it off.

"Have you eaten? Would you like tea?"

"Tea would be lovely. I had lunch before I arrived."

"Okay, good job. I'll put the kettle on, then."

Camas leads Hīnau farther inside. The kitchen and living area are one fairly small room. There are woven mats on the floor. Above, barn-style rafters carry many harvests' worth of medicine and food. Branches and stalks hang in bunches and bushels.

Camas sits Hīnau down at the table and makes small talk while putting on a pot of water to boil. The kitchen table is completely clear but for a medium-sized wooden box. On the front is a picture of a bird. Camas adds seeds to the boiling water from a glass jar. The seeds carry a strong anise smell. Warm and scented steam wafts over the living space while Hīnau watches. The water in the air wets her skin ever so slightly. Camas pulls hand-thrown mugs from the shelf for the brew. She pours it into them and puts one in front of Hīnau. They sit and hold the hot mugs and figure each other out a bit, each taking their turn to ask about family and friends in the pursuit of mutual acquaintances.

Camas asks what kind of design Hīnau would like and where, but Hīnau makes it clear she doesn't really know. Camas runs through a list of crest and clan emblems, common designs and spots. Hīnau likes the sound of the more abstract ones. She doesn't want a face or a person or a picture. She wants the type of thing her father's mother might have gotten, had she been allowed. Something simple, though when she says "traditional," Camas tells her why nothing she does can be traditional, that their definitions of such a term to begin with are troubled.

She says that skin stitching *pulls* ink underneath the layers of skin. The needles and thread are made of animal and plant fibres, bones, and sinew. Skin stitching is great for straight or dotted lines, pulling the ink through the skin with a thread. A handpoke, she says, is the deposit of pigment underneath the skin with a needle, preferably the same kind someone with a tattoo gun would use — except instead of pounding the colour into the flesh, the ink is *pushed* under the skin, one dot at a time.

Camas pulls out a small and inky pen and uses it to draw patterns round Hīnau's wrists. Parallel lines encircle her arm. In between, triangles cut together like teeth, giving the overall appearance of a closed zip or cuff. Camas sprays solutions over her workspace — strong, alcohol-smelling things. She opens the wooden box and pulls out her tools. Small bottles of ink and needles. Her gloved hands work methodically to open packets, to wrap the end of the long needle with fabric tape. Hīnau's chest becomes a little sore as she watches; she tries to imagine she is just getting her ears pierced again. Hīnau thinks of her mother, Miro, briefly. Hopes she understands.

Camas speaks in a soothing voice, checking in with Hīnau as she prepares her station.

"Look, here's the needle. It's actually several small needles, and they can only be pushed in this far."

Hīnau sees the needles crowded against one another.

Camas disinfects her arms again with a cool gel. "It's easy to stop anytime. Just say, and we can take a break straight away. It shouldn't hurt too much — it'll feel like a sore prick."

"Yup. No, I'm good."

"Any time, say anything any time."

And then Hīnau watches Camas dip the needle into the ink and bring it towards her wrist. The needle head touches the surface of her skin and then pushes through. When Camas pulls it back out, it makes a satisfying pop. Not so bad. Camas begins working in earnest when Hīnau says nothing, following the pre-drawn lines.

"Why have you decided to do this now?"

"I hadn't really thought about it before," says Hīnau, "but I visited a village site a few months ago with my cousin. I'd never done that kind of thing before, and afterwards I just felt different."

"Are you close with your other family?"

"Yeah, my mother's side — I'm definitely more familiar with them. I wouldn't say close." Hīnau thinks about her grandmother briefly. She hasn't seen or spoken to her in a few years. "But now I feel closer to whatever my father's family is — was." Hīnau winces as the needle goes in a little too deep.

"Sorry, my bad." Camas continues only when Hīnau relaxes again.

"It was strange to see the land where something happened after you've learned about it. The places where I grew up were home, and I knew things happened there, but when I learned more stories — even big, new, scary ones — the places still felt the same. Home was still home."

Hīnau's skin is already red and inflamed, following the lines Camas has drawn.

"But to see this place that was never truly home and know all the things that happened there. Bad things, old things..." Hīnau remembers the figures that appeared in the longhouse that afternoon, emblazoned on the dry grasses and fallen wood panels. The drumbeats she couldn't get out of her head.

"I can imagine. Different?"

"Yeah."

Camas works in silence for a while, and Hīnau watches the tattoo grow, as though rising up from the skin below. It begins to burn, but Camas keeps a light, dependable rhythm. The work continues until twilight, when the birds begin their talking before they go to sleep.

"I think I'm done. What do you think?" Camas takes a paper towel covered in a yummy-smelling soap and cleans the wound. The stencil washes away until it's just the design underneath the skin.

Hīnau feels something welling up inside her, but just says, "Thank you."

Camas tidies up, makes another cup of tea, and sets some cinnamon-apple muffins on the table. Hīnau eats quietly and they talk a little. Hīnau can't stop looking at her wrists. Camas walks her out to her car and makes sure she's fine to drive. They kiss one another on the cheek and promise to catch up soon.

All evening Hīnau looks at her wrists. When she washes her face before bed, she sees them in the mirror, the markings her whole family should have. She sees the thousand different women who made her, clenched between the tattoo's teeth in ink and blood.

· SAANICHTON, 1941

The children are to be taken at the end of the summer. When the letters come, they request each child by name and age. Louise sits at the table and reads them all, with the stew bubbling away in the background. Ned is still out on the boat and won't return for another hour or so. They've both known the letters are coming, but that doesn't make it any easier. At least the youngest children are barely past teething and will be safe for a few more years.

Louise hears the children outside. The house is hot and tight from the stove. Spring has just broken out beyond the walls. Bulbs are pushing through the grass and soil that clothe them, puncturing the last of the snow. The children are running up and down the dirt road full of muddy potholes.

Louise stirs the stew, tastes it, replaces the lid. In the pot the meat is being tenderized and pulled apart by the swell of broth. Sparkles and bubbles of oil and fat swirl above the liquid; bones and sockets rise from beneath. She starts on the dough for her bannock. Already her fingers are falling into stress injuries — they ache for the sting of nettles, the freshly harvested greens that bend and snap as they whip wrists and fingers. Her arms remain strong. She kneads the dough into warm and lively elasticity. There are few windows in the house, but there's one in front of the kitchen counter that looks out to the edge of the yard, the vegetable patch, the wildflowers that bloom even brighter under her care. The dense treeline beyond.

The children are antagonizing the dogs out front. Louise hears the agitated yipping echo down the road. She continues her kneading until she's satisfied with the dough's softness. She shapes it and puts it aside to rest. The birds are darkening the skies on their way home, flying all the way back from the city to roost in the forest here.

The oldest girl bursts through the door and says she's hungry. Louise tells her Papa will be home soon and then they can have supper. The girl is almost seven and looks plenty like her father, but her dark hair is cut in the exact same fashionable style as her mother. Louise makes her start washing up and setting the table. The girl rushes back outside to wash her dirty and scabby arms, before returning to pull out bowls and plates and cutlery. Louise remembers the nuns' rough hands scrubbing her, the sting of sheep dip and delousing fluid on her own skin.

Ned returns home, pale as hell and exhausted. He sits at the table and starts talking to Louise — they are still in love, and it shows. Sometimes she misses Nanaimo, but Saanich has been home for a decade now, and she has accepted the rare visits to her parents. The very few times she's had the appropriate papers to leave the reserve, past the officers keeping her in, have made her body ache with anxiety.

The rest of the kids tumble in after washing themselves in the basin. Louise heats up fat to fry the bread in. The cast-iron skillet takes on a wavering heat, the fat becoming a frothy liquid, which hisses and bubbles as the bread is added to it. The children sit around their father, who smiles despite his fatigue. He is slowly being worn away by the ocean and its hard labours.

The dough transforms from cold and pale to a crisp, golden succulence. Louise serves it with the stew and a berry jelly saved from last year. Ned eats with his eyes closed, as if hoping to live somewhere between the broth and the bread. The children fight over the biggest pieces of bannock. Louise watches the childlike ricochet of emotion and noise, which simmers down just before a fight starts.

She's seen the children who return home for the

summers between school years — ghosts who wander the dirt roads alone or stay inside all season. Louise sits at the table with her husband and children. She is thankful for the flour that made the bread, the vegetables she grows when she can, the deer Ned's brothers secretly hunt. Everyone keeps eating, and she wonders when she'll tell Ned.

ĆENITEŁOṈSET

EARTH COOLING DOWN

BLANKETS

I am in the back of my father's car. My sisters are here too, and we're driving through a small beach settlement. The houses are prefab weatherboard, rundown, with junk in the front yards. It's sunny, clear, and cold.

The two-storey houses have blankets hanging over the balcony railings. They're that kind of mink blanket Natives all round the world love. These ones have wolves and eagles on them, in red or blue. Underneath the car tires, shells and sand and glass crunch away, like we're driving over roadside middens.

We're on our way to the beach.

MOONFISH

On the first day of summer, the whole family goes to the lake. It takes about half an hour to get there, husband and wives and kids and all. They arrive in two cars. Lunch supplies have been packed, and one of the women stays behind on the sand to prepare food and take care of the babies.

The man and the other two women take the girls over to the water. The women are wearing bathing suits and big hats with sunglasses. The girls are all very excited. The water is still and green. They pretend not to notice their father wearing a Speedo, or the pearlescent burn scars across his chest. His body is upsetting and foreign.

The lake is very shallow near the shore. There's an island in the middle, where the water becomes much deeper. The edge of its shore is neatly bordered by large rocks with pockets of sand in between. On the top of the island is a micro-forest, made of a few very old trees growing together into a dense copse.

The adults take turns ferrying the girls across the water. The water never gets higher than the parents' chins, but the kids can't swim across on their own yet. When all five of the girls are on the island, the parents swim back towards the shore to rest on the sand, leaving them alone to climb up the small hill. The girls can see their parents on the opposite shore. They wave.

Then they explore the tiny island, with its few trees and surrounding views. They take turns leading each other around. They slip down the back side of the island, onto a pile of rocks that match the cliffs on the opposite side of the lake. In between the rocks is a pool of water — it's not very large, but it's deep. The water is stained brown by tannins from leaf litter. There's a faint white glow at the bottom of the pool. A fish is lying on its side underwater, its body the shape of an oval cut in half. The girls see its eye and its mouth, which is more like a beak.

"What kind of fish is it?" the oldest girl asks.

"It's a moonfish," the next-oldest says.

The children all crouch down to look closer at the fish.

"Is it dead?" A middle child swirls her finger through the water, waiting for the fish to react.

"No — its eyes are moving," another girl says. "Look."

The fish is watching them closely, following them with its eyes. Its lips move, as if it's whispering into the small pool.

"Her house is too small," the toddler says. She points to the fish and then the lake.

They all sit and watch the fish for a little longer, then get up one by one and wander off to look at other things.

Eventually the time comes for the parents to return and ferry the children back across the water. The oldest girl swims across herself, beside her mother. The youngest two are carried back first. The two middle children are left on the beach. They get restless and push each other around. It feels like forever to have to wait for their parents to make the trips back and forth between the island and the shore. The time stretches uncomfortably. The girls bicker, before one pushes her older sister away and gets into the water herself. She paddles away from the shore, out into the deepest part of the water. She's a confident swimmer; her paddling strokes are calm and even. The older sister follows in a panic, scared to be left alone. She plunges into the water without thinking and tries desperately to catch up. The water covers her neck and chin, cool and velvety. She's splashing too much. Her arms are uncontrollable, and when she catches up to the younger sister, she hits her over the head accidentally.

As soon as she feels the other girl in the water, she latches on. She wraps her arms round her sister's neck and chest, pushing her head down. The younger sister's nose and mouth fall beneath the water, and she isn't strong enough to keep them both above it.

They go down together in a tangle of limbs and violent streams of bubbles. There is messing and clawing of arms and heads. The younger girl is blond and never cuts her hair; it becomes green underwater, spreading like a cloud of corn silk. Her eyes close as she tries to get her head above the water. The older girl's eyes are wide open while she pulls the blond girl down.

They start swallowing water at the same time, cold and painful gulps of it, making their noses and throats and chests sore. They take turns gasping at the surface, trying for air and getting only mouthfuls of water. They try to scream underwater and raise their hands above the waves, before falling down farther into the deep green, the messes of eelgrass and sparkle of fish beyond.

And then they're grabbed roughly under the armpits and wrenched from the dark water. They cough and struggle, and they're still yelling. The other girls are watching from the shore, wrapped in towels and being handed fruit leathers by their mothers.

The two girls are still tangled in each other, almost wrestling, and still barely able to breathe. They're carried through the water until it becomes dry land. The adults put them down, and the younger girl is taken away to be towelled off and checked. The older girl stands and shivers. Her father bends down over her and pins her arms by her sides.

"You never push someone's head under water like that." He shoves his finger in her face. His eyes are angry and black. He stares violently, without blinking. "She could have drowned. You could have drowned her. Do you understand me?"

The girl nods her head.

"I don't ever want to see you do that again."

She nods her head again.

"Did you hear me?"

Her head is still nodding. Her whole body is shaking.

"I said, did you fucking hear me?"

The women are standing back and watching.

He is squeezing her arms so tight it feels like he could pop them off.

"Yes."

"Good." He pushes her towards her mother, who is waiting a little farther away than the other women.

They all eat the lunches. The food has the tiniest bit of sand in it, so it becomes gritty and salty. The children aren't allowed back into the water, and they play in the trees at the edge of the park instead. The girl sits in the sand and fills her pockets with it. The parents lie out in the sun or dip their toes into the water.

Then they load everything back into the cars and drive home. The highway cuts through the forest, concrete snaking back towards the city. The girl pretends to fall asleep on the drive so her father will have to carry her inside when they get home, sand spilling from her pockets.

WOODY

1.

Around here we teethe babies on salmon. Pa brings it home in bags from village smokings. Our uncles catch the fish, flay and debone it, then spread it over wooden skeletons that hang above the firepit. It becomes dry and chewy, like jerky, and dark red-brown — the perfect thing to give to a baby cutting their first teeth. Hard and soft, smoky. Even when we have no money, we have this.

2.

Very few times, Pa and I go out alone together. Usually, we're on the way to the dentist in a different town. When it's time for lunch, we might stop at an A&W. Pa likes these places because they serve root beer in big steins. He orders his favourite burger, the one with bacon and onion rings on it. He orders one for me too and asks if it's good. Or maybe we stop at the English-style chip shop on the highway with the ice cream cabinet. The flavours are outrageous, like bubble gum and tiger tail. Pa orders chips in small baskets. He sits me up at the bar counter by the window and goes to fetch our food. When he returns, he has a bottle of vinegar and a bottle of ketchup. He douses the chips in the vinegar so they're steaming hot and wet. Eating them makes my mouth feel like it's one big wound.

3.

It's powwow season and the sun is harsh. The field is crowded with vendors and visitors. We're allowed to wander and look at tables of merchandise. The grass is dusty and dying. Some of the dances have started and the drums are going. Pa has a feather in his hat. We crowd round a food stall, and Pa buys us corn on the cob. It's been cooked in tin foil with butter; we each take a cob to eat, bursting the kernels between our teeth. Later in the summer we'll be shucking the corn ourselves, making corn husk dolls in the backyard.

FOREST

The air is thick with water. The trees are so tall we cannot see their tops. Every surface has something growing on it. Earth and wood are covered by a woven moss blanket so heavy it must be peeled away in layers. Salamanders pull themselves along slowly, following the trails of yellow slugs, their skin speckled brown like ripe bananas.

From the canopy, hanging gardens reach down, impromptu ferneries that keep the roots of seedlings warm. Cedar bark has been harvested in long strips, revealing creamy interior flesh. Other trees nearby bear wounds made by cougars, which go only deep enough to reveal rich red. Cedar stumps rot and crumble into fecund sienna. Huckleberry bushes sprout up from the mulch.

Pitch a tent, rest a while. The still water is not so far ahead. In another time we would have spent the day here, making our offerings, and taking medicine and food home. Now there's a path and a sign and a railing to guide us across the gully.

The forest stops suddenly, pine needles giving way to monolithic stone. There's a lake bottomed by stones so big there is no sand or earth to be seen. The long and smooth rocks meet one another under clear water, paving the floor of the lake. Huge American bullfrogs float below the surface, their long toes barely brushing ancient stone.

STONES

Pa opens a Canada Dry ginger ale. He's lying on the couch, and my sister is balanced on his belly. She's still fresh — tiny but chubby, and smilier than circumstances should allow. Her cheeks press up into her eyes, which are black and wet like a seal's. Pa goes away during the day and comes back much later, so this quiet time is our only time together. He keeps his life a secret from us, and keeps us a secret from everyone else, even his own mother. Pa sips his ginger ale and watches us with a hard stare.

After he settles in, I get up and show him a rock I found on the beach earlier. The stone is glossy and black and completely smooth. He makes a sound of recognition, and then I leave him alone.

Every day we get up at dawn and go for walks — all of us, my sisters and their mothers too. We walk along the beach on the reserve and all pretend to be friends. The beach is made of rock rather than sand. Turning over stones reveals small but ferocious crabs. They swarm like wet, earthbound bees to safety under a new rock. The water is too cold for swimming, but sometimes we dare to pull treasures from the lapping edge to feel the sea for ourselves. The forest impinges on the shoreline, and eagles drop from the treeline to fish. All around us small islands close in.

When Pa returns for the day, I know to be quiet and more reserved. He opens a can of ginger ale. In trying to quit the bottle, he's giving himself diabetes.

A few months later, Pa takes us to a beach with a gift shop nearby. He doesn't interact with us much, but he likes to take us places and show us things. The shop is full of scientific entertainments for kids — and bins of gemstones. We're allowed to buy one each, which is a big deal, and I take too long to decide. There are plenty of contenders, and Pa comes up behind me as I weigh them against each other.

"This one." He picks up a small triangular stone, opaque and milky grey. "Agate. It's your birthstone." He drops the stone in my hand. Parallel stripes run across its surface. It's smaller and less interesting than the others, but it's the one I take up to the counter to buy.

The agate sits on my bookshelf, next to the black stone from the beach. I've hung up a picture of my grandmother an aunty sent me on Facebook. She is young and looks upset, but she's really pretty. Towards the edge of the photo is an empty beer bottle.

THE CABIN

Salal lies by herself on the pier. The sun has come and chased away the early morning mist. It's getting hot; the early summer brings hovering blurs of heat across the island. The planks beneath Salal absorb the sun, frightful splinters of burning that sting when they touch the backs of her thighs. From the house she can hear the clink and rattle of metal hitting china. Alba is inside, tidying up their lunch dishes. The sunlight follows the ripples across the lake, the trails of circles made by waterfowl. Salal shields her eyes and rolls onto her side and keeps reading her book, leaving the sun to brown her skin.

She wakes in a panic. She hadn't intended to fall asleep. Later in the evening Salal and Alba are holding a dinner party for their friends. They have already spent a week at the cabin by themselves and wanted to do something they could invite their friends to. This is the place Salal's grandfather owned and worked as a fisherman. She is lucky her uncle let them borrow it for the week. It's a gorgeous spot now, modest but tastefully renovated since Salal's family really started making money. Alba is still new to this island, unfamiliar with its wilderness. Salal can tell she's excited to be out here. It has been achingly hot all week, but Alba has insisted on wearing Red Bands around the property, just in case.

Salal starts to worry about the timing of this evening. She wants to will herself to get up and go inside, but feels paralyzed. The sun has made her skin angry and pink. She should get indoors to avoid further burning, but she stays lying on the jetty slats. The sun beats down in parched waves. Her tongue won't even move to lick the salt sweat off her top lip.

Loon calls out on the lake. Eagle nests above, in the tallest firs. Their sharp cries echo along the surface of the water and the hills behind the basin that the lake rests in. Salal watches the birds fish all afternoon, then return to their nests and clean themselves. They shake out their feathers before biting and pulling them back into place. She watches until Alba calls her inside to help make a shopping list. The spell breaks, and she finds her fingers moving again, her arms pushing up the rest of her body. She knows it's happening, but she can barely feel it. Salal leaves her book and blanket on the wooden slats, waves lapping so slowly and softly beneath them, barely audible.

As they discuss dishes to make, Salal begins to feel a little dizzy. Alba is a competent and quick cook. She knows what she wants to buy, and basically just wants to run her ideas past Salal, who doesn't want to go to the supermarket at all. She doesn't like supermarkets, or the way the flickering neon overheads make her feel, but decides to go anyway. She can't decide what to make for dinner, and this way she can see what is good and fresh to eat. Alba has a few small appetizers she wants to make, finicky things with very particular ingredients. Salal hopes that seeing the fresh ingredients nesting in their intricate pyramids will give her ideas. Her skin is sore and her chest starts to freeze up. As it gets harder to breathe, she gathers her wallet and phone and keys — and refreshes her email several times, pulling the window down over and over again to search for new correspondence. She's not waiting for an email from anyone in particular. They get in the car, and Alba slams the driver's side door loudly. Then they're on the open road.

As evergreens zip past on the drive into town, Salal feels her body tense back against the seat. Her feet flatten on the floor, as if she could push down hard enough to slow the car. At every corner it feels like they won't turn in time, even though Alba is a careful and considerate driver. Salal flinches as cars pass them. Alba squeezes her knee softly and tries to distract her. Salal imagines her grandfather opening fish with his knife, cracking and splitting their ribcages into flat skins, leaving the ripe flesh spread pinkly underneath.

The supermarket hums and buzzes. It's relatively empty, which should be comforting, but it seems to make every interaction with another customer or store worker even more jarring. The air hums with the sounds of freezers and air conditioners. Out front of the store is a solitary beggar who is being asked to leave by a weedy security guard. Inside, women with expensive, cropped hair buy organic farm-raised salmon. Salal wants to move quickly through each aisle, looking at only necessities. But Alba insists on asking employees where things are. All of the produce here is local and grown on the island. Alba loves this.

Salal tries to decide between different greens for a salad. Arugula or spinach? Her mind volleys back and forth; she comes up with pros and cons, trying to imagine the different fixings she would use with each.

Alba comes up behind and rests a hand on the base of Salal's back. "Having some trouble?"

Salal looks up and is sure Alba sees her empty stare and panicking mind. "Yes. I want to make a salad."

Alba pretends to think for a moment, and then says,

"Rocket is your favourite, right? Why not just make a salad of your favourites?"

"I want it to be special."

"It will be special. What's more special than cooking the things you love most for your friends?"

Salal's mouth turns down a little. "I don't know."

"Here, we'll just get the rocket. There's a thousand things you can do with it, and it's more flavourful than spinach." Alba picks up a nice bag of arugula and puts it in their basket. "We can always come back if you change your mind." She kisses Salal's forehead and pulls her on.

They pick up easy things: some cured meats, soft cheeses, a baguette. Alba has already found all the stuff she wants to cook with. Salal looks at the fresh fruits, nuts, and seeds. Tomatoes and peppers in reds and oranges and greens and purples. Alba helps her choose nice things, even if they're more expensive. Salal feels guilty and worries about eating them later.

Back at the cabin, the afternoon whittles away into arranging food on small platters. Everything can be cut into tiny geometric pieces of itself and reconstituted with other ingredients as something new and transcendent. Salal tries to focus on the exciting alchemical aspects of cooking, the transformation that division and heat produce. She peels a cucumber into careful, even ribbons. Beside her, Alba is confident and happy in the kitchen.

Something continues to feel heavy in Salal's chest, drawing down painfully. She rests her arms on the counter in front of her, lets the sharp wooden edge press into the flesh of her forearm. She concentrates on this sensation — the hard, bruising feeling. The new counters are made from recycled timber from around the property. The surfaces are all warm red-orange. A mask carved by Salal's uncle hangs on the living-room wall behind the couch. It's a legendary bird with a long and strong beak. The mouth pieces of the mask have been made so the beak can be opened and closed at will, with loud and hard *clack-clack-clack*s. Legendary Bird stares at Salal while she watches Alba chat happily, julienning vegetables into fine sticks.

Throughout the cooking, the weight on Salal's chest only gets heavier. She tries not to let her mind run in circles, but it does, and she starts to feel paralyzed again.

"Can we go outside for a bit?"

"Of course." Alba understands that something isn't going well for Salal. She takes her hand and leads her out the door. "Would you like to go for a walk? Round the edge of the lake?"

"I'm not sure." Salal can see other people walking on the lakefront — tourists and holidaymakers. She's a holidaymaker too, but only in the same way her ancestors spread down to the south shore during summer in the old days. She isn't a disruption for simply visiting here. Regardless, she doesn't want to run into anyone on their walk. "This way." She leads Alba away from the busy shore.

They take the track up to some of the old stones. It's not long before they see the tall rock face covered in markings. These are the only petroglyphs Salal has seen on the island. She knows there are more elsewhere, but these are the ones closest to her family. To Salal, they look like snarling wolves. There are fish too — sole-type things — and a few human figures. Tourists come in the summer and take photos or rubbings. Alba is almost in disbelief when she sees them. Salal has neglected to mention the archeological marvel that rests behind her family's summer cabin. When Salal tells Alba the approximate ages of the petroglyphs, she gasps. Alba is very excited and asks if she can touch them. Salal shrugs and lets her know that everyone else does. The rock has been carved into smooth, rounded lines. Salal used to come and sit with the stone when she was younger, leaning against the rock face for hours, reading or drawing. Little wolf figures running across the page, their tongues and teeth out. She wonders whether she should have brought Alba here. She didn't think about it before at all. But she banishes the thought as Alba touches the rock, tenderly almost, avoiding the carefully carved lines, as though she might smudge the marks someone made three thousand years ago.

Dusk falls slowly. By the time it's dark, they're back inside and Alba is lighting the fire. Salal hands her the lighter and matches and stands back to let her conjure the flame herself. The wind races through the chimney and makes howling sounds, blowing smoke all through the living room. Then yellow headlights illuminate the driveway. Two carloads of friends arrive at once, Alba's workmates and Salal's friends. The weight from earlier still sits below Salal's ribs, but hearing her friends laugh and shout from the car makes her smile. Salal and Alba greet them all on the porch, beers in hand. Everyone piles inside with ornate salads, bowls of fresh and fragrant food. Marguerite has baked a cake.

"How's it been, being away together?" Hanna sucks on her tiny vape.

"Great. I guess."

"I guess?" She coughs out a cherry-flavoured cloud. "You've only been dating for three months! This is meant to be the most romantic time of your fucking life."

Salal looks away. "I don't know. I've just been feeling weird lately."

"Like skipping Zoloft weird, or…?" Hanna's thin eyebrows rise comically high.

"Like there's a lot going on at the moment, and I feel like I barely have any energy or time to give Alba."

"Sure. Relatable. That's just grad school, baby."

Salal's lips press together. "Yeah. Maybe it's more than that. I don't know."

For a second it seems like Hanna is going to press it, but she knows Salal won't have any more to say. She splits the difference. "It's a bit of a shame. She's pretty sweet."

"You say that like you're surprised."

Hanna just laughs.

Alba is in the kitchen with her friends. When she relaxes into happiness her face takes on a childlike quality, as though her joy is unencumbered by other emotions. Sometimes Salal wonders if everything feels simpler for Alba.

They all eat the food in a Dionysian spread across the small table. The dining room is more of a breakfast nook, but they've filled it with sumptuous dishes — extravagant salads, where several of the main ingredients are not vegetables. Alba made inappropriately small crudités, but they seem to delight those who eat them. Someone has brought candles and someone else collected wildflower posies. Marguerite's cake sits in the centre of the table. It is black forest, layered and tiered and delicately frosted. She has carefully placed maraschino cherries along the top, the kind that are so sweet and pink that even the stems burst into syrup when you bite into them. They eat to the point of pain, though Salal isn't very hungry after the afternoon of cooking. She feels happy to see her friends like this, but still needs another beer to even begin to relax. She breathes in big gasps, releasing her hoppy breath into Alba's face. Someone else dims the lights.

It is later that Salal starts noticing the wispy threads of blue light that follow her friends' movements. Hanna reaches for her drink, and the bluish smoke follows her arm. As if it's heavier than air, the smoke falls to the ground in misted drops, pulling a silky thread of vapour from her sleeve.

Kaya and Marguerite are dancing, and when Marguerite raises her arms above her head, Salal can see tiny pin feathers pushing through her skin. As if in time-lapse, the feathers extend and harden, cased in keratin, until they outgrow their casings and the dead matter falls to the ground. The feathers take a breath and settle, a brilliant teal, as primaries, secondaries, tertials — the trailing edge of wing.

Kaya is laughing, her wide mouth opening farther and farther back. Her mouth is a bear's mouth, wrapping round her head. The teeth inside sharpen momentarily, before rounding down. Behind them, where Alba was standing, is a small berry patch. Her vines and bushes shrink and grow, blooming and fruiting over and over again in front of Salal. There's a small shimmer of light across Alba's branches.

Hanna is watching beside Salal, clapping a slow rhythm. They sit together until everyone who was dancing has transformed in front of them. Salal turns to say something to Hanna, but she has become a skin drum and a padded drumstick — all the animal dancers in front of Salal keep time to Hanna's beat. The pain in Salal's chest becomes stronger with every strike of stick on drum; the twisting pain splits her heart and echoes in aches through the rest of her chest. She has to get outside.

She puts her beer down and gets up to leave. As she closes the door, she looks back at the dark living room. The pulsating blue light reflects through the window and onto the water closest to the cabin. There is the faintest sound of waves lapping the shore. Moon has risen; Loon calls out on the lake.

Salal sits on the jetty's edge and remembers every visit to this lake. The stops at the ice cream parlour on the drive down. The silence and mists of dawn. Fighting with her sisters in their canoes. Sitting alone with the rock in the forest.

Then she remembers getting ready to canoe one morning with no one else around, just her father. He helped her into the yellowest of life jackets. The water was still and black behind them. Salal was scared of falling in — falling to the bottom. Her father clicked the clips on her jacket and yanked the cords so hard he crushed her chest. The pain sat between her ribs and jumped out towards her heart and lungs. He pushed Salal towards the canoe and turned to his own jacket. She remembers not being able to breathe.

SK̲EK̲ĆES

My sisters and I visit their grandparents — their mother's parents, who are strangers to me. Both are carvers and make their grandchildren gifts by hand. Each of my sisters has been given a sort of Cabbage Patch doll made in their own likeness. The dolls are made of fabric that has been stretched, buttoned, ruched into human forms. I have come along but receive nothing.

After the gift-giving, I feel Pa's hand on my back, and my sisters and I are pushed outside. The yard opens up into forest. We're told to go looking for red huckleberries. The forest has retreated where it touches the property's carving paraphernalia, and in some places the ground is covered in cedar sawdust. There are enough clearings and piles of junk that we do not get lost in the bush. Pa and my sisters' mother linger behind us. The grandparents stay in the house.

We collect the berries happily. They're bright and

perfectly round; the sunlight shines through them. Unlike salmonberries and blackberries, huckleberries are not made up of drupelets. They are one single bead of a berry, so red and shiny that they look like gems.

Once we have enough, we go back inside. The house scares me because of all the art on the walls. Smoothed cedar mouths pull back into grimace smiles — painted red, blue, black. They are watching me, looking half like people, half like spirits. Masks and carvings with hair and teeth scare me the most. The house is small, a dark two-storey cabin. The light inside comes from tiny windows in the kitchen that look out into the forest. We eat the huckleberries with vanilla ice cream, and then we leave.

SAANICHTON, 2002

That year they have Christmas in the dark. They huddle in the middle of the living room, and the adults give the children their gifts. Things like Terry's Chocolate Oranges and Kinder eggs, which the children are more than happy with. There is delight in cracking the oranges into their predetermined slices or doing the same with the eggs, splitting them down the seam. The toys inside have small parts and plastic bags the adults are worried about. There are a few toddlers this year, not to mention the baby, who has received the best gift of all: a real toy, a white stuffed bear that could pass for a Beanie Baby.

Though the room is dark, lit faintly orange, the girls get to work assembling the toys from the eggs. There are puzzles made of cardboard with only six pieces, or plastic figurines of characters from TV shows they don't watch, which require little assembly. The baby is sucking on the toy bear's ear. Salal is holding onto her while they watch the others complete their tasks. The baby spits up, so the bear is covered in the sickly sweet-sour of undigested breast milk. The baby and the bear get taken away and cleaned up, before being returned to her big sister.

It feels like nighttime, but it's the morning. Later they'll go for a walk along the beach and spot eagles and the car that has McDonald's toys stuck all over it, or build small and dirty snowmen on the side of the road — it snowed on the reserve in the night. The baby and the bear will go everywhere together, so much so that it still smells like spit-up years after.

RETREAT

Now

Star slops champagne into the glass. It splashes over the lip of the flute and darkens the white tablecloth. Cedar doesn't care. She pulls her jacket closed round her chest. It's made up of the tiny pelts of martens and minks. They wrap her arms and wind up behind her neck. The wind blows bitter from the north. Lush berries bob in the flutes of champagne; they make an orange blush. The table is out in the courtyard, next to the creek, which talks and talks as they drink.

Star holds a glass out to Cedar. "Cheers, babe."

Cedar takes the glass and knocks it against Star's.

The clink is lost in the sound of the chef putting down their meals. "Ladies." His pale hands set the plates in front of them — gleaming white circles. Piled in the centre are steaks of smoked salmon. Oils and nettle greens have been mixed into a rich sauce like a chimichurri. Swept through the sauce and resting around the steaks are maple blossoms, small green shoots that resemble hops. The man tidies the table, dabbing at the spilt champagne.

"I'm famished," Star says, pulling apart the pink flesh. "We've been working up an appetite all afternoon."

Cedar smiles tightly and starts to eat.

After the meal they rest and watch the sky dim into evening.

"We've lost daylight," Cedar says. "Would you like to keep working or are you tired?"

Star stretches. Her head tips all the way back; some of her vertebrae crack dully. "I'm a little tired."

"We could do some small studies in the meantime."

"All right. Why not?"

Cedar stretches too. Why not?

They take their leave of the table. Star goes to check herself out in the bathroom mirror, to practise her contortions and stillnesses. Cedar passes her on the way to the studio and sees her tensing the muscles in her face, changing its shape and edges. The studio is at the end of the hall, where the house is somewhat elevated. The ground is a few feet below. In the outer half of the room the walls are windows; Cedar added the extension after receiving a commission from the

Met. The room opens out into dense trees with mossy trunks. Epiphytes fall and drip, branch to branch. The light is a filtered white and green.

Cedar arranges herself and her materials. She hasn't been able to paint for the last two months. She hasn't talked to Star about it, and so they've carried on as if nothing is amiss. Studies and drafts are easy. There is nothing hard about producing an image, a feeling, a particularly satisfying shape. It is even easier when using Star to leave impressions on a page. At this point it sometimes feels like Cedar is paid just to watch her lover pout and twist in front of the tall windows, ancient forest standing behind.

The heating turns itself on as it gets darker. Cedar breathes in through her mouth and alternating nostrils, using finger and thumb to block the opposite nostril. Then she stretches and winces, feeling the troublesome tendons in her arms and hands. At twenty-seven, her body is already deteriorating. She has watched her family fall apart at much younger ages, in much more dramatic ways, but the injuries and tensions of her hands make her feel as though she is slipping into the same inevitable pain.

Star enters the room with a sigh, her hair freshly braided, wearing a soft cotton robe. "What are we doing tonight?" She sounds almost bored. A year ago, she was enthusiastic and professional.

Cedar spins back and forth on her stool and turns the lights up a little. "Whatever you feel like. This is just foundational work."

The robe slips from Star's shoulders as she stretches her arms above her head. Her breasts are small and tipped with conical nipples. The falling fabric reveals her rounded belly and strong thighs.

Watching Star move and pose has long ensured that Cedar knows she herself is unattractive. It is more than apparent during sex, but to come into the studio afterwards and watch the ways that Star has been physically blessed is agony. Cedar can feel every ounce of flesh on her body and the way it pulls her down, closer to the earth. She knows Star pretends none of this matters, that she doesn't notice the ways Cedar's cheeks sag to jowls, or the denseness of her flesh, the roundness. Cedar has never had children, but her body looks as if she's had several and never bounced back to nubile beauty.

Star begins to pose beneath the overhead lights. Below her, several shadows spring up and follow her movements in unison. Cedar starts sketching and feels her physical discomfort fall away.

Not all of Cedar's work comes from this live modelling. A lot of it is based on detailed reference pictures. She has thousands of printed photos of Star. Macro images of her skin, her hair, the bold ridges of her toes.

Cedar takes all of this into account as she paints. The slip of oil and pigment churns into the red-brown of Star's skin, the greens and whites of her eyes. Cedar takes particular care with the blackness of her hair, the wispy baby hairs that soften into her eyebrows.

As the colours dry, they lighten and blend into one another. It is only after the final layer of varnish — dammar gum dissolved in turpentine — that the colours are reborn, brighter and clearer than before. The resin gives a wet-slick-live look. Star loves to stand behind Cedar as the varnish is applied. She loves watching herself rise to the surface of the painting, as if the tip of her nose or bottom lip could be touched by brushing a fingertip across the linen canvas.

The forest grows dark behind Star's twisted body. Cedar changes the programming of the light, to illuminate a little more of Star's shape, but it has grown so dark that most of the drawings will become large swathes of charcoal dust.

"How are you feeling, dear one?"

"Tired," Star says. "Hungry."

Cedar lets out a big breath and feels her body relax a bit. "Well, I suppose we should eat again, then."

Star breaks her pose and lets her arms drop. "Thank you. How do things look?" She comes over to the workbench to pick up all the studies and sketches from the last few hours. She holds up the pages and looks through them, still naked and stunning. Not a lick of shame on her.

Star kisses Cedar behind the ear. It feels good — hot and cold at the same time. Cedar rolls over to face her in bed. It's Saturday morning, and the sun is out. It's winter, but the light is warm. Star is pushing her thumbs beneath Cedar's shirt and feeling the weight of her breasts. She presses the folds of skin, slick and sweaty from the sunshine. The sheets are soft and muted colours. Cedar's hair is freshly dyed and has a delicious smell, chemically clean and beautiful. Star obviously wants to have sex. Cedar tries not to think about it.

Sex used to be exciting and shivery enough that Cedar forgot herself until after it was over. Then she would feel the inadequacy and weight and worry. In the moment, Star touched her with reverence and kindness, and Cedar tried to concentrate on sensation — feeling and taste guiding her more than vision. Later, in the same bed, Cedar would replay the event in her mind, trying to imagine how she must have looked and felt. There were a thousand unpleasant parts of her body, and even more angles from which to view them. The slight bump and rise of sebum in her skin. If she looked at her skin in the mirror for too long, she could find those thousand things to bother and squeeze, all of which turned to angry red sores afterwards. She hated the holes in her nose, the deep pores that filled to the brim with oil. She hated the fine hair on the sides of her cheeks. Most of all she hated the ugly shape of her face, the scrunched and rounded quality of it, the jowl and second chin underneath.

But the money changed things, no matter how much she had hoped and expected it wouldn't. Soon there was enough that spending it regularly wasn't an issue. There was a house, a mortgage that was promptly paid, further renovations. When she discussed her career, people seemed surprised she made any money. They wondered how she managed by simply selling her paintings. Cedar had ample funds to have clothes fitted and tailored, enabling her to avoid her own figure. There was much less time in the day than before, and diets became impossible under the pressure of tight work deadlines. No matter — she had several people she could call to whip her up a pair of perfectly fitted culottes and matching blouses. The fabric and garments could be completely handmade and dyed naturally, with traditional dye techniques. The tailoring could be perfect enough that Cedar could pretend she felt differently about herself. It hid a multitude of sins, as did the elaborate skin care routines, dye jobs, gemstones grown in laboratories, and time for ceremony. None of it really changed the chemistry in her brain or rewired the traumatic synapses that fizzled with self-loathing. So Cedar settled for feeling like an ugly burden with a private chef.

Cedar watches Star's face carefully. She's looking out the window and posing, but her robe on the ground has started buzzing. Cedar sees Star pretend not to notice. It's raining outside, the patter of rain drowned out by the insistent buzzing. Behind the windows, mist rises from the forest floor. Birds come out to forage in the rain. The edge of Star's garden is beginning to creep into view. Beans have crawled over from their appointed plots, climbing the wooden beams of the house. Cedar tries to shake off the irritation of seeing the garden and its exotic bounty impinging on the forest view. But she can still see the vines in the corner of the window — the scarlet flowers beginning to die off.

Star's phone keeps vibrating.

"What is that?"

"I'm sorry, I left the vibrate on." Star looks pale.

"Do you want to go and turn it off?"

"Yeah, I — sure." She crouches down to check her phone, smiling quickly before she turns it off and slips it in her robe pocket.

"Do you need a break?"

"No, I'm fine." Star stands up and resumes her pose. Outside, the birds continue their fussing.

Star sighs and rolls over in bed. Cedar is curled in the opposite direction, pretending to be asleep. She knows Star is awake. Cedar breathes deeply and listens to Star move around. The bed sinks and bounces as she stands. Cedar hears the phone charger being pulled from the socket, the bedroom door opening, the car starting in the driveway.

Then

Cedar manages a move to the city by herself. She's seventeen and has the dedication to make it to art school and get scholarships and work afterwards. She's tired and lonely in a new way but manages to keep pushing through small victories that lift her up and make her crash afterwards. A string of good grades, important one-off jobs, a friend who offers her part-time work at a framing house; they follow each other once Cedar puts her heart into her work. She takes her art seriously in a way she hasn't before — the city is alienating and harsh, but each week there's something new to see, a thousand different people creating art and sharing it with the public. When Cedar meets Star, she wants to create her own spectacle.

It is a pretty gloomy day, the coastal skyline falling down close to the earth. Cedar's days have been split into those that are productive and those that are spent entirely in bed, barely eating. At that moment it's an almost even split between the two. Some of Cedar's work is beginning to really get noticed. *There is something exciting here*, one buyer said, and Cedar could feel it too. But she knows she hasn't quite hit her peak yet, so there is a momentum, a reason to keep going.

Cedar is on her way to the framing house to visit her old friend Tania. She was one of the first people to help Cedar out with her career. Tania's workshop is in the centre of the financial district — a strange place for it, but she also owns the coffee shop that sits inside. On weekends the entire building is empty, which is why Cedar only visits on Saturdays. The buildings nearby are all glass, and the sun bounces off them in blinding rays, even with an overcast sky.

As Cedar opens the door she hears a hearty laugh, the kind of aunty laugh that pulls her straight back into childhood memories.

"Tania?" Cedar doesn't much feel like talking to anyone else right now, or talking at all for that matter. But she has a painting to pick up, so here she is, fresh from a three-day stint in bed.

As Cedar rounds the corner, she sees Tania sitting at the front desk, coffee in hand. She is sitting across from a woman Cedar has never seen before.

"Cedar!" Tania says. "Morning! How lovely! Star, this is my good friend Cedar. Cedar, this is Star." Tania waves a hand between the two women.

"Star, good morning." Cedar takes Star's hand and kisses her on both cheeks. Star is tall and willowy and dressed in a linen blouse, camel breeches, and equestrian boots. She holds herself in a very compelling way.

"Hello, Cedar. This is so exciting! Tania was just telling me about some of your pieces that made it into my favourite gallery." Tania winks at Cedar.

"Yes, it's all been very intense. I have — I've come for that canvas, Tania. I don't want to hold you up for too long."

"You're not holding us up. I just made coffee. Come — come on, silly. Sit." Tania pushes a stool towards Cedar and goes to fill a mug from the coffee pot.

Cedar sits warily, aware she might not be able to escape for some time. She can smell lavender and coffee steam. The concrete floors are carefully polished. Cedar rubs the heels of her shoes together.

Star smiles a bright, genuine smile.

• • •

The first time Cedar paints Star, there isn't time for thought or doubt. Cedar arranges her things and chats happily to Star, pretending she isn't nervous. The form that springs up from the canvas is supple and clear. Cedar is surprised by the image. It appears different from her usual work in small ways — an ethereal liveliness in Star's eyes, the delicacy of the hair on her body. It's exciting for both women, and Cedar decides to start a whole new project, just the two of them. She does all of her preliminary work, speeding through reference sketches and underpainting. Something about the project consumes her, and her days fill with thoughts of Star's body, in and out of oils.

Cedar starts waking in the morning with thoughts of work swirling round her in heady clouds. While she waits for breakfast to be made, she sits at the kitchen table, cup of coffee poised in mid-air. She stares at the light that hits the walls, the soft morning light with dust motes and shadows from cedar branches outside. She takes long, long baths in the evening, steeping herself in hot water and tea tree oil. The water slicks over her skin and sore limbs. Her whole body gives her grief, she thinks. Most of the time anyway. Sometimes she passes a window and sees the curves of her body — more pronounced than other women's — and so she doesn't hold it against her body. She indulges in clay masks and refreshing lotions.

Cedar undertakes her nightly skin care routines and makes her plan for work the next day. She makes it through a whole month in this way, without a single day in bed.

Star stays for dinner most nights.

Then it's the opening night of Cedar's first big solo exhibition, and she's running late, because she knows she doesn't look like she should. Star arrives to help coax Cedar out of the house.

The evening is a blur, and Star bears the brunt of the attention. She is the woman in most of the paintings — life-size oil canvases of wild women on cliffs, in woods, in streams. She looks the part of muse, tall and draped in a silk gown. Star's dentalium earrings drip down onto her shoulders. Cedar fades behind her in a black, collared shirt, a turquoise bolo tie. They make a strange pair. When people come up to talk to Cedar, their eyes wander across to Star, no matter what Cedar says.

The night goes on, and Cedar's clothes become uncomfortably tight and hot. She downs her drinks a little too quickly. Star hangs off her arm all evening and, as they leave the gallery, declares the event a success. She stoops to kiss Cedar in the cool night air. Then they go their separate ways.

What follows is a week in bed for Cedar. She dodges the calls and messages from her friends, even her family. She talks to the chef through the bedroom door and gives him a short list of groceries to pick up, along with instructions to take the rest of the week off. She shuts everything out with a harsh firmness. Several of her paintings sold on the opening night of her exhibition, but she can't get excited about that at all. Every person who reaches out about it — the gallerist, Tania, even Star — makes her chest tighter and tighter, until she feels like she can no longer breathe.

She watches the weather pass through the forest, slowly and with a lighter touch than it would on the coast. Often there is a fine mist, or slight rays of light that penetrate the dense thicket of redwoods around her home — the only signal of what is happening in the world beyond her cabin.

A few days in, her back starts to ache from holding the same positions. Cedar falls into shakes even thinking about seeing another person. This is the kind of time she wishes she had a pet to keep her company. She has to settle for the birds and squirrels out the window.

• • •

What finally makes Cedar get out of bed is the fear that one of her cousins might turn up. She would hate nothing more than to be caught in the midst of a bed episode by either of them.

Cedar props herself up and looks around the room, before opening the windows and trying not to fall back into bed. She checks her phone, which has been on do not disturb for days. She has several missed calls from art contacts and friends. She makes her way through the voice mails and begins to feel physically sick. The last one is from an art dealer who wants to talk residencies, commissions, nominations, and money.

After returning a few of the calls, Cedar goes to eat for the first time that day. She makes herself ramen, with all the different seasonings in small foil packets. She knows she shouldn't eat such things, but in times like these it's often all she can bring herself to make. She boils water, which fogs up the window, and empties all the packets into her little bowl. The noodles boil over, and she drains them before adding them to the sauce. She mixes the noodles wearily and takes them to bed. She eats and watches a woodpecker against a tree trunk.

As soon as the food hits, she feels her stomach turn. She eats quickly, but the damage is done, and her insides begin to cramp up. Since she was young, she's had the worst stomach aches, usually from dairy, but now they follow other things too. She's made a mistake eating the noodles. They squirm in her belly, their oil upsetting her stomach. Cedar lies down and pulls the blanket over herself. If she had the energy, she would make herself a peppermint tea to calm the nausea and pains. She lies still, so as not to agitate her stomach, and begins to worry. Instead of being encouraging, all the messages that people left on her phone have exhausted her. Before long, her chest falls into the familiar tightness of anxiety. Tomorrow she will have to leave the house, to carry on. Cedar has plenty of things to look forward to — professionally, personally — but none of it feels like it matters. The only thing she can think about is how to stay inside the house, away from all the people trying to pull her out.

Before

Cedar was born fat, like most babies, though there was something extra to her weight, the folds and creases of her elbows. Her mother, Arbutus, was delighted to have such a daughter. As an only child, Cedar was adored and coddled. She performed a thousand happinesses and laughters for her mother, who wore herself thin to keep them in their home — wherever that happened to be at the time. Mostly Cedar grew up on the reserve, where the peninsula jutted out and she could see neighbouring villages both north and south. Arbutus took all kinds of work but nothing that ever made much money. They were together and happy, and that was all that mattered, whether or not they lived in a trailer or a motel or the basement of someone else's house.

Evenings would be spent at the kitchen table together. Arbutus would write or do some work, and Cedar would sit across from her, drawing or painting. Sometimes there would be the tiniest bit of money left over at the end of the week. When she could, Arbutus would use this money to buy Cedar's coloured pencils or tubes of paint, the occasional pad of thick watercolour paper. They would work quietly near each other. But as dawn rose, Arbutus would be back out to work again and Cedar would have to get herself to school.

Sometimes she wouldn't go at all; instead she would visit her grandmother, who would lead her through the forest and show her what to eat or use as medicine. Her cousins lived with the old woman, down the gravel road. Cedar saw them often enough but was scared of them. They were older than her and had been born when things were very different for their mother. The oldest liked to play games and tricks on Cedar. He made her confused and self-loathing. Sometimes he locked her away in cupboards or tool sheds, and her other cousin just watched and laughed.

When she escaped back home, it was to an empty house. She would look out the small windows, which never let any direct sunlight inside. Though the house was kept dark, she could sit and imagine small pictures — images and colours that sprang up from the dust of pencils. She would draw botanicals mostly; it was the quiet hum of plants that she loved dearly, branches of Salal berries or the beautifully fingered leaves of devil's club. Sometimes she would tear a page from her notebooks and paint it a graduating wash of reds and browns, like arbutus bark.

When she did have to go to school, the days became long and hard. The other kids jabbed and pulled at her body. Cedar felt alone, behind, out of the loop. She would come home and sit on the bed and look at all the pictures she had pulled from magazines to draw. She would lie down and feel defeated and cry, but she was never quite sure why. Arbutus wouldn't be home for a few hours. Cedar would let her stomach grumble and hide in her bed, alone, until her mother returned.

WEXES

The abalone shell is tucked into the corner shelf. This is where Pa puts all his precious things. He'll rest his turquoise belt buckle there, his hat, the new age books with pastel purple-blue-indigo covers. Eagle feathers rest nearby. They're the length of my forearm and creamy white; farther down, the fibres of the feather turn to brown stripes. The abalone shell is dusted with ash.

My sister and I sit on her bed and look through horse books. Her favourite horse is a palomino — they're blond like her. My favourite horse changes all the time. I worry the skin on the side of my fingernail and watch her turn the pages.

"Can we go see the frog?" I ask her.

She says, "Sure," and we exit the trailer.

Pa picked me up earlier in the afternoon for a visit. My sister came for the drive too. On the way back to the reserve, she told me that she had a pet tree frog. It wasn't kept in a tank like I imagined. Instead, it stayed near their trailer, in the bush.

She takes me out back where they shower some-times — and there she is. On a particularly tall and skinny tree is the tree frog. She's bright, bright green and has her body folded up against herself. She smiles and blinks, slick skin shining. My sister picks her up and shows me closer.

ĆENQÁLES

HOT EARTH

MAUNGANUIOTEAO

They're driving to visit a city up the island. They pass
the old volcanoes — two, if not three, of them — on
the way up. The land falls away to sparse space rock
and tussock and middling road. Lumps of widow-
makers perch atop trees, which start to look quite
unlike the ones they're used to back home. The whole
stretch of road is different. They make the journey
due north until they see a sign for the national park
and turn off. The trees start to change after fifteen
minutes, firs and milled pines turning into red or
silver or mountain beech. They show their age, even
from far away. The car is following the road, which
is following the railway line. They pull over at the
Last Spike. They park and get out, embraced by the
cold and fresh. This earth is volcanic rock and ash
with heather growing through. The air around their
ears feels different — the atmosphere, the altitude,

the feeling like maybe they aren't even on earth anymore.

They decide to follow some tracks left by a car through some broom, back towards the ravine they passed on the way. The track is gravelled mud with pūkeko tracks running through. The bird's toes are so long and sharp — perfect for bullying juvenile mallard ducklings, rending breast and down, ripping off beaks. The tire tracks end at a picnic table, a small clearing, an empty fuel canister, a pile of rotting sheep worn down to the wool, trash dumped from the nearby farms. They stop at the carcass, say sorry, and pass it on their way towards the lip of the cliff. The train tracks sit beside them, coloured with rust and built on wood and jagged stones. They hear the faint sound of water running, and then they're at the edge of the earth.

The stone wall on the opposite side of the ravine is dripping with kiokio, green ferns tumbling all the way into the river. Trees are unsure of the bank and sudden drop; a few brave ngaio and tī kōuka make a go of vertical rock. Several mamaku wind up and down, following sunlight and mists.

They stare down to the river moving between the rocks. The railway track moves across each side of the earth and the air in between.

• • •

"How long do you think it took for the river to wear the stone down that far?"

"Fucking ages."

They both try to breathe better. It feels like a waste not to breathe this air properly.

"Wow."

"Wow."

One of them toes the edge of the stone, dislodging some small pebbles. They fall through the tight layer of ferns straight into the air and, several long seconds later, the water. The drop is completely vertical. They both look over the edge, feel the gravity.

WHAEA

"Kia ora, Whaea. E pēhea ana koe? Sorry I haven't visited for a while."

That's fine. You've been busy. I've seen you running in and out of the whare all week.

"I missed you, though."

I missed you too. What have you been up to? I thought all your classes were finished for the year.

"They have. They finished last Thursday."

So what's been keeping you busy?

"I've been going out onto the water with a girl from class. She likes to go fishing."

You don't eat fish, Nīkau! Have you been sticking them yourself?

"Sometimes. I don't like it much, but I enjoy being out on the water with her."

Is she beautiful?

"Very. She's clever and funny as well."

I'm happy for you, girl. Does she know much about you?

"Of course, we've been in classes together all year."

Hmph. Where's she from?

"She's European, I think. Her parents have been here for quite a while. They're citizens and everything. I met her in my introductory reo lessons. She loves the language."

Enough about that. Tell me how the end of school was. What are your plans for the summer? Are you staying here or going away while you can?

"I wanted to ask what you thought. I have a little money saved. Mum thinks I should stay and save some more, but I think I might like to go somewhere."

Where would you like to go?

Nīkau waits outside her gate. Around the gravel path a cloud of dust erupts, and beneath it is Ilse's van.

"Hey!" Nīkau waves her hand. Her shoulder is starting to hurt.

"Hello!" Ilse sticks her head out the window. "Kei te pēhea koe?"

"Oh. Ah. Good. Pai."

"Kei te pai ahau."

"True, sorry." Nīkau shifts the strap of the bag that cuts across her back.

"Get in! We're already late, e hoa!" Ilse hops out of the driver's seat and opens the sliding door. She's already tanned, even though it's barely November. "Would you like a hand?"

"Yes, please." Nīkau hands over the bag of tackle, and Ilse takes it with ease. Her body twists with slight muscle. Her ashy hair is in a ponytail, and her eyes flash an unnerving blue.

"We're going to have a beautiful time today! I can just feel it!" Ilse says.

"I'm glad. The water is so still today. We're lucky."

"Is there such a thing as luck in a place like this? It's always this stunning!"

Nīkau looks around the bay. Behind them hills carpeted in bush tumble into the ocean. There are only gulls in the sky. The sounds of children swimming by the dock float over. She doesn't say anything else.

"Let's go! Get in, e kare."

The sliding door slams closed and echoes loudly.

The boat rocks, and Nīkau is unnerved. She's exhilarated to be out on the open water, but senses too the danger that sits under the waves. She's never believed in any god, but any time she enters the ocean there seems to be an inevitable drag and pull, a force that's inexplicably alive. She's aware of the agency a current can have, aware that the ocean could choose to push her under, roll her across sand or rock, crush her under the weight of a thousand tonnes of water.

Ilse hums and laughs and catches fish. Her eyes squish shut in happiness, and her clean, straight teeth peek out from behind her lips.

Nīkau lets her fingertips brush the top of the water, slip beneath the surface. The water is silky and temperate. It's the kind of blue water that arrives in the sounds only during summertime. Beyond the prow of their boat it sparkles where it meets the horizon. Nīkau is grateful and wishes she could find a way to thank the water. She imagines fish of all sizes rising from the bottom of the ocean to nibble her fingernails, the fleshy pads of her hands. She wants to fall into the water and be picked clean by the smallest fishes, have her skeleton worked over by tiny crustaceans. Nīkau is hopeful that one day she could be sand.

They arrive back at Nīkau's house in the late afternoon. They put the fish over some ice and have a cup of tea. Ilse has visited a few times already, but still examines all the photos Nīkau's mum keeps up around the house. Every aunt and uncle and kuia have made it onto the old house's walls.

Ilse takes her tea with whole milk and sugar. She points and asks, "Who's this?" at several of the photos, and Nīkau explains, feeling flattered that she's interested in her family. By being interested in her whakapapa, she must be interested in her too. Nīkau makes a point of standing close to Ilse as she explains the lives of the tūpuna in the pictures.

Ilse takes her hand as she talks, and Nīkau stumbles in her stories. Ilse kisses her cheek, and they laugh. They take their tea to the porch and sit down.

Several days later Nīkau asks impulsively, "Would you like to meet my favourite aunty?"

"For sure! I would love to! Where does she live?"

"She's in the graveyard outside of town."

"I'm sorry, I didn't realize she had passed."

"It's fine. It hasn't been a year yet. I still visit her often."

"Was she your mother's sister?"

Nīkau says yes and offers to drive them there this afternoon.

The overgrown grass waves in the wind. The urupā is on the road out of town, towards the highway. The women hold hands and walk through the graveyard.

Nīkau introduces different, more distant family members on the way to her grandparents' plot. Some of the spaces are missing grave markers, and headstones aren't necessarily where they usually might be. The wind gets stronger, making them both squint.

"Here," says Nīkau. "This is Nanny and Koro." Her grandparents lie side by side.

Ilse notes the dates. "They died quite young?"

"Yeah, I suppose they did."

Nīkau looks for her aunt. She rests right beside her parents. Her headstone hasn't been unveiled yet, but the small marker for her grave is gone. Nīkau walks round the plot but finds nothing. "I can't find her. She's meant to be here."

"That's strange. Maybe someone took the marker?"

But Nīkau knows that isn't the case. She looks around the graveyard but stops herself from calling out. "Sorry, I brought you here for nothing. Let's head back."

"I can't believe you hid from me!"

Yes, you can!

"Why would you do that?"

You know why. I didn't like the look of that girl.

"Well, I do!"

No, you don't. You're just bored here. She's nothing special.

"I've been having a really nice time with her, actually. I wanted you two to meet. She's really interested in our family."

I'm sure she is. You know what those people are like. Some things are better kept to ourselves.

"I would like to be with her, though."

That's fine, but it won't last, girl. Get your head on straight. She just likes the novelty of you.

"You can't say that!"

It makes her feel better to be friends with you, like she's experiencing the real, authentic, traditional —

"You're being a real bitch right now, you know that?"

Oh, bub, get over it. Come summertime she'll be gone freedom camping with her mates.

"Maybe I would go with her if she was on a road trip!"

You hate camping, Nīkau.

"No, I don't!"

You'd rather piss yourself than pop a squat. You get carsick. There's no Wi-Fi or phone reception off the beaten track. Face it, girl, it's not a good match, eh?

"I only said I would maybe go! Stop pretending you know what's going on in my life — you're not here anymore."

You know I wish I was.

"Yeah, I do."

You should do whatever you want this summer, Nīkau. Well, whatever that bloody sister of mine will let you do.

"I don't want to leave home before I have to."

Then stay.

WHALING

Down by the bay, where the stormwater drains rush into the sea, the sand grows all kinds of funny things. Errant pumpkin seeds sprout in the sand because it's wet and hot. There's a view of the small offshore islands where they keep birds safe. There used to be women who lived out there with their husbands, who were whalers or warriors or adventurers. Later on they were farmers. There are houses dotted across the steep landscape, small shacks that sit at the foot of the mountainous peak of the island. If you were on the beach of such an island, instead of this one here, you would easily be able to see anyone approaching from the north or south. Any direction really. This is especially useful when you have just fled from your homes and are slowly sowing yourself down the coast, hapū by hapū.

If you were married to a whaler, you might expect to

pass your time by softening flax with a mussel shell, or later a metal tool. You might be able to sit around with the other women while the men hauled their catch up onto the land. The smell of the rending fat would carry on the breeze from the big boiling pots. As the coils of flax rope grew and night arrived, someone might start drinking. Over the fires people might all start singing the same song in different parts. Someone might come and lift the work from your hands and lead you away to dance. Come morning the men would all be back out at sea, with the exception of your husband, whose head belonged to the man who kept you all safe from the dangers that followed you down the island.

FOOD

We get the permit on Wednesday, so on Saturday we're able to make our way up into the hills to find something good to eat. I'm trying to see all the new treasures I've missed on walks before, like the tender hearts of cabbage trees and hen and chicken ferns — the kind we grow at home but always forget to water, so the leaves become dry and translucent but spring back into succulence with a hearty drink.

I especially love the rhizomatous ferns and spleenworts. They move by themselves through the undergrowth, make their way up tree trunks if they so desire, and feather off the wood like ostrich boa. There aren't really any berries here, especially not at this time of year, but we are surrounded by bitter and herbaceous plants — Jurassic trees that stretch their new growth away from the earth, to keep their fresh green hearts away from giant birds.

We put knife to branch, stalk, stem; smell fresh weeping sap; put catch in the appropriate bag. We keep the dog on a leash to avoid poison traps for pests, but she pulls and whines at the sounds of birds snapping twigs in the distance. There is a dense, acrid, sour taste; light falls in thin shafts through tops of tree ferns. Above, sky runs quickly, cloud passing over canopy with shaky speed. The wind sounds, but underneath such trees it is just a gesture of wind, a faint howl.

Kaikōmako flowers fall onto muddy track as tiny perfumed stars. The whole forest is sweet musky springtime. Tawa berries drop — fat, oily olives — from finely leaved branches. Orchids push up through the earth beside the path, fresh shoots with unusual flowers yet to open. You need to meet a tree just once to remember the different ways it can be your friend.

After the rain the streams are heavy and fast, falling down the earth towards the ocean. Farther along the track are the dried-up beds of older streams, slopes of rocks the same shape and size, like foreign burial mounds. The clay around the water is covered in growth that's hard and green and scaly. The root systems of punga colonize the waterway, fresh roots growing into the still water in the ditch.

This isn't the place we thought we would end up, but it's the only way to heal the things we're hiding from. I crouch to snap a leaf or branch, thank the plant, be grateful for the weather and the car that got us here, and for waking up today. The small treats we take home to consume are the things that will keep us going for the rest of the week. Sometimes I feel weak and fragile in a way I'm certain isn't physical, but I appreciate being able to try to fix myself in such a corporeal way.

We carry an assortment of bags and jars and knives. We take very little of any one thing, except for when the tarata blossoms with heady lemony bursts of flowers — then we pick as much as we can carry from the towering bushes to take home and soak in gin.

It makes plenty of sense to me now, but for a long time it didn't. Each no-dig hāngi we make in the oven with cabbage leaves sutures a different part of me back together. Every time we collect and cook something together, with love and joy, makes up for every time I ate until I was sick. We take a small moment each day to stand in my parents' garden in the sun. To nourish ourselves, we harvest the earth and the beings that spring from it. All our small attempts to care for ourselves and each other wash away some of the shadowy figures that have followed us around for so long.

I have a knife, a basket, and two legs. He kai kei aku ringa.

HE WAHINE AHAU /
EHARA AHAU I TE WAHINE

Pūhā lies back on the doctor's table. She spreads her legs and feels the cool air between her thighs. The doctor is chatting away, trying to soothe her nerves. The doctor is nice but doesn't seem to understand that Pūhā doesn't feel apprehensive. Now that she's here, she doesn't feel anything at all. Pūhā hears metal on metal. She prepares herself for the feeling of something inside of her. Her breathing is steady.

A womb is a world of problems. A Greek man from a thousand years ago might try to convince you that a womb makes you crazy. As Pūhā feels the speculum enter her, she thinks that her womb has only ever been a resignation. As a child, bleeding at first felt like a death sentence. She didn't understand that the blood came only once a month. She took the menstrual pads her mother handed her and resigned herself to bleeding every day of her life she had left.

The doctor spreads the speculum, and Pūhā feels a sharp pain. She'd thought she was prepared, but as the doctor pushes farther, it becomes apparent she was not. The doctor swabs her cervix, and Pūhā thinks about how much she hates the pictures she has seen of such parts. They're pink and look very sore and sensitive. She hates to imagine a whole baby being pushed from such a thing.

On the months she bleeds, the cramps radiate out from her spine, through her back and belly. It used to make her feel like a real woman. She would cuddle up to her ex-boyfriend and complain and know that, even if the rest of her life failed, she could have his baby and maybe then her life might mean something. Pregnancy scares were wonderful. They were among the most powerful reasons not to kill herself.

The doctor withdraws the speculum, congratulates Pūhā, and begins to tidy up. Pūhā gets dressed and slips her shoes back on. She thinks about visiting the wharenui at her marae, the shoes lined up outside. Men were supposed to enter the whare first, and women should follow. Because of their child-bearing abilities, women were to be protected. They held the future of the people in their bellies. Pūhā feels uncomfortable with this — she would check her womb at the door if it meant she could find her place freely and without judgement. Though she found warmth with the aunties at the marae, she still felt a distance from her assumed womanhood.

The more she thinks about it now, the more she does not want children. She spends most of her mornings staring out the windows of her small flat, the glass heavy with condensation. Sometimes it takes her an hour to begin to make breakfast. She falls into despair. She wakes tired, ready to die. Recently, her uncle gave her a little dog he found in his neighbourhood. That has helped. Pūhā takes it for walks in the morning before she eats. The dog makes her do anything at all.

The doctor is describing how tiny cysts grow in and around ovaries. Pūhā is wondering if she has no reproductive abilities whatsoever. If she can't have children — the children she hasn't planned for and doesn't want — then what is the point of the womb that burdens her so? She imagines splitting her belly open and stepping to the front of the line — standing among the men on their way inside the marae. Maybe it wouldn't have been so fraught for her before the foreign ships came.

Maybe her friends and family would have understood her, known that there was something different about her body and who she loved, and celebrated her gifts. Whether she had a womb or not, maybe they would have never quite treated her as a woman. And maybe that would have been more comfortable. The doctor hands Pūhā some freshly printed documents on PCOS. The paper is still warm; the ink was running out and gets lighter on every page.

The doctor is explaining Pūhā's hormone level results. Her testosterone is higher than a woman's usually is. This doesn't sound so wrong to Pūhā. She feels like more than a woman. She loves being a woman, especially one who loves other women, but she is uncomfortable with the idea that this is all she's meant to be. There is something else inside of her, for sure; she's just not completely clear on what, or who, it is. She is a woman dwelling between worlds of shadow and light.

They say that women are the land; the earth is a mother. Pūhā is not the earth. She does not feel formed from the clay at Kurawaka. She feels like the sun: scorching hot. She feels like Tāne's legs and thighs: taut and tired. She feels like the swell of ocean water. When she dies, she knows the birds and lizards and ugly fish will cry a din. She is a trick, a locked door, the disembodied laugh of a ghost in a hallway. Physically, she carries the burdens of te whare tangata, but she has made decisions, and the Creator has made decisions, that mean she will never bear children. This is acceptable to her.

The doctor shakes her hand and leads her to the door. It feels like Pūhā leaves something behind in the room, on the examining table.

DOVE

The day of the wedding, her mother comes over to do her makeup. Mahuika is beautiful. Her lips are full and love to smile and gossip. Her hair is in perfect, tight curls. She is seventeen. She is three months pregnant. She wears white.

The groom is Pākehā and a few years older than her. He comes from a large family too, made up of severe teetotallers and older brothers in the army. His youngest sister adores Mahuika and her throaty laugh. For years to come they'll chatter away in the parlour of the old house by the river like small and noisy birds.

The service is simple, but the sky is blue and Mahuika has a beautiful sweeping kind of feeling that washes over her. Her father is proud and jolly; her mother sits beside him, watching carefully. Mahuika begins to shed a tear and turns towards the camera.

TANIWHA

There's a taniwha in the museum. It stalks the temperature-controlled alleys at night and slides open drawers of taonga on smooth rollers. Greenstone weapons rest in hollows of styrofoam, their shapes traced and cut out, giving the appearance that the treasures are level with the edge of the tray.

The taniwha removes the metal bars used to quake-safe the archives. It has long fingers and claws that wind the wheel of the moving shelves open and closed. In between genuine articles are fakes, displayed in the exact same fashion. No overt features distinguish them as fakes, they just are. There are casts of taonga from overseas that are made from plaster of Paris and painted in acrylic. When the taniwha knocks against them, they make a hollow sound. The museum is often making replicas of things.

The taniwha opens a set of drawers filled with

flags from around Aotearoa. The largest was flown at Waitangi when they signed Te Tiriti. It was handed down through a single family and repaired over and over. Darning has been done by hand with red wool. Later someone took pieces of fresh crimson fabric and sewed them over the holes with the zigzag setting of a sewing machine. Eventually someone else wrote the whānau's name in big block letters across the centre of the flag with a marker.

The taniwha likes to hide things in the drawers, where they shouldn't quite be. The taniwha talks to the pou that come back from all over the world. Some are so tall they make the belly drop. They were carved so long ago that it's clear the trees don't grow as big now as they used to do. Some are painted green from their time at Wembley. This taniwha hasn't left the country yet. Its parents hope it will go on an overseas trip to Britain after this.

The taniwha can often be found doing paperwork at a desk in the middle of Collections at night. The human staff swipe in and out of the storerooms all day, so the taniwha waits until they go home to start its own work. It may process some of the recent acquisitions or reply to international inquiries for taonga. The taniwha may take breaks in between paperwork to look at things, open the drawers, and touch all of the korowai and kākahu. Kiwi feathers fade over time if exposed to light.

Where beams of display lights hit the kākahu, bleached and dull stripes appear. Muka that begins white always fades to yellow.

Sometimes, just for fun, the taniwha will twist the pokinikini off a cloak or piupiu. It pulls out the secret feathers that weavers hide in the body of their cloaks, the ones stuck in backwards. Huia, kākāpō, ruru. It pulls the hidden feathers out one by one and places them on its tongue, to be melted away by its acid mouth. Sometimes it eats its lunch from the hākari bowls: piles and piles of raw fish, some still gasping for oxygen. It carries the hākari bowl through the collections, ripping the heads off the fish and sucking out their insides. Its long and unkempt nails click on the linoleum floor, its heavy tail dragging behind with a scratchy weight. Sometimes it lets other taniwha look at the taonga. It likes to impress, and it thinks this job is very impressive.

The taniwha guards the taonga jealously. Other taniwha often try to swap treasures, taonga for taonga. They have things that come from the ice, the jungle, the desert. The taniwha would like to have some of these things too, so it will negotiate a trade. A taiaha for an oil amphora, a coin, a tomb. It visits the online collections of other institutions. Sometimes they're not allowed to take photos of their taonga, so they'll list the content itself. Rattle. Rattle. Coffin. Rattle. Mask. Grave. Basket. Rattle.

WAIKAWA

When you go home, across the bay, you have to take the big commercial ferry. This is the easiest way to make the journey from one island to another, and back again. The water is blue — strangely so. Dolphins chase and scatter. Hidden in the pockets of land masses are tiny houses, with small jetties to pull into. The water turns to white froth where the hulking metal cuts through it. Behind, large trails of still-churning water follow the ship. The harbour is left behind quickly, the lighthouse, the smaller islands. Then the ocean is open — for hours. Only much later in the day does land reappear. Unrecognizable bodies of earth erupt through the salt water. The ship pulls through and turns, righting itself towards an invisible harbour. And then, all of a sudden, you're in the magical sound. The hills billow and fall around you. The land is soft, soft green and the sun is warmer. The breeze from the strait falls away and it becomes bearable to sit on the top deck of the ferry. The ship pulls into the dock, so you clamber downstairs, through the wet Atlantic chill of the basement of the ship. The deck is wet and slippery and growing things. Now you can drive off into the summer heat of the bay where your ancestors landed two hundred years ago.

THE SIGHT

The year Mahuika turned thirteen, they had to leave the bay. It'd been their home for two generations already, and the whenua had always cared for them as best it could. The hills up behind their house were full of plump birds and heavy berry bushes. It was easy to head up into the bush for the day and return with enough kai for a week. In the marina, seafood was still plentiful, though not as much as her kaumātua's tales suggested it was before. When sailors used to land and wade through the blue water, it was almost impossible to find any ground to stand on — it was so covered in spiky kina. There was bounty across the land, if one knew where to look.

Behind this veneer of natural beauty, life in the bay was harsh, even on its most stunning and glorious days. Though some kai was bountiful, plenty of the whānau in the area were very poor. Looking back later, Mahuika was able to understand why her mother had wanted them to leave. The old houses rotted and crumbled round their inhabitants; children were always sick. There wasn't much beyond what you could catch with your own hands.

But when her mother had first broached the subject, Mahuika had wanted to scream. She wanted to make a scene and shout that she would stay in the bay on her own. There were plenty of friends and whānau she could live with. Her parents could move on without her. She fought with them often. On the night before they were due to leave, they were still fighting. It was Mahuika against her parents and siblings. There was something in the land she just couldn't leave.

After dinner and further argument, she ran out the front door. She was in her sleep clothes, running down towards the dock and the bay. Her feet were bare, their flat and wide soles making heavy thumping sounds against the earth as she ran. There was a feeling of injustice inside her. This was supposed to be happening to someone else. Mahuika had never minded watching the misfortune of others, but if anything ever happened to her, she felt as though the universe was conspiring against her specifically.

Behind Mahuika the lights of her parents' home glowed softly in the dark. She could see the sparkling black ocean. It was dark and very cloudy, hiding the new moon away. They hadn't built street lights on the marina yet. Mahuika ran farther out on the jetty, towards where the ferry docked. Tomorrow morning, before the birds awoke, her whole family would be here, with all their possessions packed into the car. Her brothers and sisters would line up and wait patiently to board the ship.

Mahuika stood on the edge of the jetty and looked down at the water splashing at the wooden supports. When she looked up again, towards the horizon, she saw a small blue ball of light hovering above the water. It appeared to be very far away. Mahuika felt the wind grow stronger, threatening to push her over. The ball of light grew bigger and bigger against the black horizon. It shone brighter and brighter before bursting into a full spectre. It was a ship from a long time ago, a European one with sails and a hulking frame. It was moving faster than Mahuika would have expected. The whole ship was made of blue light, the darkness visible behind its glowing outline.

Mahuika's heart stopped. As the ship got closer, she could see people moving around on the deck. The ship pulled up alongside the dock and threw down a gangway. Everything was silent, except for the rushing sound of waves. People began disembarking. Men in old-timey clothes like miners or sailors would have worn a hundred years ago. They were talking and working quickly, but Mahuika still couldn't hear them.

One of the men walked towards her. He was built like her brothers: thick, heavy, and strong. He was carrying a barrel across his shoulder. He wouldn't look her in the eyes. He walked straight through her. Mahuika's mouth watered with nausea. It rolled down her body and made her hands shake.

In her mind she saw where the people on the boat had come from — the same maunga as her own whānau. She could see all the things that made them flee, and it made her want to crumple to the ground. Her head filled with the sights and sounds of death. Terror struck like rapturous lightning. She watched men capture and torture children. The women and girls were raped, and the men were shot through the head. The pā was on fire. It ate away at the houses, the food, the farm equipment that ploughed the fields. The maunga sat behind the village silently. There were men in uniforms, grabbing whomever they saw fit. Some were on horses, some had muskets. The fire spread; a child's hand held up a piece of bread, a feather, a poi. A few managed to flee, but most were arrested. Hundreds of them.

The men and women who disembarked from the boat had lived through this. Now they'd made their way here, slipping through Mahuika on their way to land. Their hearts were heavy, but there was relief too.

They were safe for now. Soon their stomachs would settle for being off the sea. It all washed over Mahuika. Her head started to hurt. She watched the children run towards the land. A great blue sun had risen over the night, and they played underneath it, hiding in the trees that lined the shore.

A woman stopped to stand in front of Mahuika, her hair flaming under the blue sunlight.

"Can you see us, girl?" she said in te reo Māori.

Mahuika's tongue was stuck to the roof of her mouth, so she just nodded.

"How funny. What's your name, then?"

"Mahuika."

"Mahuika! You seem too meek to be a Mahuika. What secrets are you keeping under your fingernails?"

"None. Nothing."

"Well, you can see us landing here. You must have some secrets, if you're able to see the dead."

"You're dead?"

"Āe. For a long time. But here we are, and you can see us. What brings you down here at this time of night, in the darkness of the new moon?"

"I was angry. Māmā is taking us away from here."

"From this beautiful place? To where?! Your mother must be a foolish woman."

"She's not! We have to go somewhere else. Things are too hard here. She wants to go back up north."

"What's up there for you? What is better than this?"

Mahuika blushed. "I don't know."

"Well, be careful. The waters were furious on our way down here."

"We'll be on a big ship. It'll be fine, though I don't think we can control it anyway."

"You can try your best. You're here talking with spirits, nē? You make sure to say the right karakia over the boat before you leave. Now, go home to your mother. Accept the journey that is coming to you. We all have to leave home sometime, even under the worst circumstances."

Mahuika shook her head and turned to leave. The blue-red woman drifted through her, towards the shore. Mahuika's body sickened with ice. Then she was running from the marina, back up to her house, never once looking back at the boat that was being unloaded.

In the morning she helped pack the car silently. The whānau drove down to the ferry terminal and boarded the ship. Mahuika tried to think of the right words to say over the boat. She settled for a karakia that was somewhere between the old world and the new. She bowed her head and muttered away before boarding with her parents.

◆ ◆ ◆

She didn't see another ghost until her father died, in their new house, on the new island. She woke in the middle of the night and saw him leaning over her, his wide frame an icy blue. He stooped to kiss her forehead, and her heart dropped. Then he laughed and was gone.

ĆENKI,LES

———————

EARTH BORN AGAIN

CONCEPTION

they say the first man fell from the rain
or broke the sky apart from the earth like an axe /
    through tōtara

they say that it was a woman,
or a bird, who opened the box that let all the light
    into the world

they say that it's your fault
what transpires in the womb
that acute maternal stress in utero leads to children
with mood disorders or ADHD

they say if you want to hide, you must make yourself
    a raincape of flax
or cedar, and fling it into paru to rest and become
    black as moonless night

they say that the smoke of plants can cleanse you, a
    dry smouldering branch
or water on the embers, crouch over the steam

they say the universe flips and swivels to reorient
    itself, no matter what you do
for instance, you couldn't stop your parents meeting
no matter how much you wanted to
they would always snap back together like elastic
    bands
for at least a moment

ARCHEOLOGY

I am building a garden with my wife. She is only just becoming herself. All around the yard my father has planted trees like a neurosis. Horopito and kawakawa line the fence; kānuka brush springs up where other plants are too fussy to grow. Some of the trees are pets and receive special treatment, but all are fed and watered regularly.

The yard is more sand than earth, and planting anything requires a heady dip of fertilizer. My wife wipes the sweat off her forehead and straightens her headscarf. Inside, the dog is asleep. My sister is in her room working. I don't know where my parents are, but it's okay.

We're digging a disused section of the lawn. Under the mat of grass is sand. Sand and the occasional stone. My wife digs the hole and I supervise, less familiar with the shovel than she is. While she pulls up masses of gritty sand, I think about where we'll plant what.

There's a dull clink; the metal of the spade hits soft rock. My wife stops and steps back. We lean over into the hole to see what we can pull up. Our hands and fingers go in, digging carefully. I feel something hard and porous and lift it out.

It's a long leg bone. I place it on the ground.

"Do you think there are more?"

We go back in, feeling for the pointed tips of bone. Instead of digging them all up, we level the earth over them, brushing it away. A whole skeleton begins to appear, rising from the sandy ground.

The body is curled over on its side, as though we have disturbed its sleep. The skeleton was a short person. The bones glow an unearthly blue. We keep brushing away sand and uncover a pelvis and ribcage. A spine snakes down the right side of the body. Then comes the skull. Smaller than I would have thought.

I sit back on my heels for a moment and see what we've done. Blue smoke rises from the bones in wisps.

I decide to keep removing the sand. I uncover stone tools, a jade adze, a wooden totem, an ashy cloak. Tangled round the spine is a necklace of a two-headed serpentine figure. Without thinking I reach forward and grip the cranium. It comes away easily from the spine.

I bring it up to my own and see the curve and fall of my own shaved head. The teeth are wonkedy and have an overbite, just like my own before I got braces. I turn over my skull in my hands; I look through the eyeholes at my wife. The world is a blue haze through them.

The teeth jut out, and I pick at them with my thumb. I can feel my own thumb in my mouth, running over the molars, a fingernail slipping between two teeth. I see my small body in the hole, the invisible weight of flesh on its frame; I feel the warmth of the sand over my skin, a blanket of earth.

Next to it are the remnants of my own life: a waterskin, a leather-bound book, and small, sharp whalebones bound to sticks. The treasures dearest to me. The cloak underneath my bones is a dirty white, but dusting it reveals white and soft feathers — kōtuku feathers. I resist the urge to run inside and bring out my paintbrushes. My wife stands farther back, in shock. I want to stop and think about what I'm doing but I can't; I just keep pulling up taonga, gorging myself on them.

I'm practising archeology on my own body; I'm constantly looking back into the hole. And I am greedy for the taonga beside my body, hidden in this land when it was a swamp. I tuck my skull under my arm, to dig up other treasures.

APOCALYPSE

It's the end of the world. All of the islands are on fire. All around the women are people falling down dead. They look at one another, these women from across centuries, and find small glimmers of themselves hiding in one another's forms.

"What shall we do?" one of them asks.

"There is nothing we can do," another answers.

The women wait for one another to speak again, out of politeness and deference. Behind them the sea rises as a giant wall of salt water. In slow motion it grows taller and taller, until it blocks out the sun and plunges the women into darkness.

"What we can do," the youngest of them says, as the wave crests and curls above them, "is break the issue down into small and manageable pieces. I often write lists or bullet points —"

"What the fuck are you on about, bub?" says the woman with the musket.

Another mutters, "What a load of rubbish."

The water begins to fall, first in droplets — singular splatters — and then a shattering pour. The women take one another's hands. Some of them aren't wearing any clothes. Some of them are wearing clothes they made themselves. The rest are wearing clothes made by slaves from other islands far away.

Then the water is rushing down, hitting them like a punch to the head. Their noses burst furiously with bubbles. The water stings in their nostrils and throats, but still they try to open their eyes. They can see each other through the blue at the bottom of the ocean — a hundred women who were once part of the same human fabric.

They all try to talk at once, bubbles pouring from their angry mouths. They refuse to acknowledge the weight of the water above them, the water that rises higher and higher and starts to crush them. It feels like pressure in the skull, in ears, in other cavities. It feels like an awful headache, like not being able to think anymore. It begins splitting their bodies open, breaking their bones and bursting through their flesh, until the water is red and rich, and all the fish swim happily towards their bodies, hungry for the floating entrails.

MOTU

SILE and I sit out on the northwest tip of the island. We watch the fog roll in and out as the sun plays above the water.

"There," SILE says. "That's it." Her arthritic finger rests on the horizon.

I can't quite see anything yet. SILE's eyes have refused to lose their sight, and they prove their ability even now, over my younger, shrewder ones.

"What is it?"

"I think it's a boat — big and tall, ungainly. But still coming closer."

"What do we do?"

"You are going to warn them, over there." She turns and points behind us with her chin.

"Is that allowed? Will they let me go?"

"We've all agreed already."

We sit and look some more, and the shape moves,

though I can't tell whether it's coming closer or not.

"What should I take over?"

"Whatever you would take out on the water anyway. And take extra clothes for warmth."

I nod. The other island lies closer to the cold south wind that drags across the ocean. "Do you think I should be worried?"

"No."

SILE stands up, and we start walking home.

We return to the longhouse, and I start packing. TÁN hovers behind me like a hummingbird. In her arms are treats she usually tucks away for wintertime. I open my satchel, and she hands them over and tells me to pack them carefully. There are dried berry cakes, honey, dried salmon, and oolichans in their grease.

"Are you worried, TÁN?"

"No, I don't think so. We have all discussed it, and I know SILE wouldn't send you away, over there, without good reason." TÁN sounds truthful but still uneasy.

I don't say anything, just keep packing my bag. I add small tools and stones, the pieces of cedar wood MÁN has been teaching me to carve.

TÁN lays her raincape beside my bag. "You might need this — for the mist in the morning."

"Thanks." I fold it lightly and leave it next to the satchel.

The dogs run around our feet and between the fire and our laps. They're excited by the smell and sound of the food I'm packing away.

I pick one up and let it wriggle in my arms. "I'll miss you, dear one!" The dog smiles, in need of a good brushing. I feel the soft, clean hair of its coat, which mats together so easily into beautiful yarn but needs vigilant maintenance. I hand him to SÁĆS, who settles down next to the spindle and starts combing out the loose and knotted hairs.

The night is getting colder, but the air in the long-house is warm and thick. Fires burn in each family's corner. Aunties take turns telling stories about the island across the ocean, the emancipated relations there — their ways that are so unfamiliar and differ-ent to ours. They are the children of the man who wrenched apart the darkness. I have heard all the stories before, but I try to pay better attention, to try and understand what they mean and what they can tell me about where I'm going. The stories are poetic, allegorical, melodramatic. I wonder which bits are true.

SILE quiets the gossip eventually. She starts drum-ming and singing about strangers and omens and sisters separated by oceans. The smoke from the fires fills my nostrils, and I feel my eyes begin to close. I fall asleep to the final wavering notes of SILE's song.

The fires are still burning at dawn. Outside the

longhouse a mist hovers along the ground. As the sun begins to leach through the treetops, the water evaporates into the air. Gold light touches the fresh leaves and moss, awakening animals and people alike. I spend the early morning checking what I packed last night. The sun continues to rise and warm the earth. I wear TÁN's cape anyway, anticipating the wind chill on the water. Everyone else rises slowly, until I have checked my things twice and the mist has gone.

My uncles leave to pull out the canoe I'll use to cross the sea. TÁN and MÁN are holding each other as we walk towards the water. My smaller cousins run through the bush, following us in parallel behind trees and rocks. SILE walks beside me, not saying anything. We reach the lip of the ocean. The sand is dry, and the tide is out. The rocks click against each other with a brightly metallic sound. The ocean rushes towards us and falls away. There are no birds in the sky. I wonder if I am too late.

"Take these." SILE holds up three loops of dentalium shells, strung between dried berry beads. "In case you need gifts to give." She lifts my hat and pushes the necklaces down over my head.

I start packing my satchel into the canoe with some fishing tools, just in case. An uncle hands me my paddle. I hug SILE, TÁN, and MÁN, and push my boat out into the water.

"HÍ,ÁȻE!" my family shout. It's a quiet day, and their voices carry across the water for a long time, but eventually drift too far behind to hear.

The sun warms my skin as I paddle. My breath takes time to come because I'm still sleepy. The stories and songs in the longhouse lasted for a long time last night. My dreams were filled with everyone's voices, shaped by their anxieties and wonderments, until I felt the apprehension rising in my belly. At times I slept, but it felt like I was awake and waiting for dawn, my mind running with a thousand things to do and no time to do them in.

The water cradles my canoe as I try to work up a rhythm. The island across the water is barely visible on the horizon. Clouds hang low against its shape. My arms and chest start to warm up, and suddenly my paddle is cutting through the water with ease. A cormorant dives for fish in front of me, its oiled body folding into the water. When it finally resurfaces, we are several feet apart.

The sky is beginning to blush by the time I pull into the outer reaches of the bay. It has taken a whole day of paddling to make it across to this place.

The waters close to each island are peaceful, and the currents and tides are regular and friendly. But the open stretch between the islands is deceivingly difficult to traverse; the water pulls and pushes against itself in unnatural ways. Currents carry you north or south when you're trying to paddle east.

When MÁN was teaching me to paddle we came out farther than usual, and he showed me how you could be pulled far away, towards the ice, if you weren't careful. MÁN told me about the being who lives in the bottom of this water, who hungers for human company, who pulls unwary fishers down. He showed me how to lend my weight to carry the canoe through the danger.

I am exhausted.

And then the water is a brighter blue, and the sand beneath is lighter. This new island is cloaked in cloud and low-lying bush. Smaller islands lie on either end of the bay, beyond the edge of the shore. My body is sore and tired, but I need to get onto land before darkness falls. I pick up the pace a little, pushing forward. It helps to think about the food in my bag I can eat when I land.

As I get closer, I can see the beach is sandy and smooth and leads up into tall dunes. Thin grasses line the lip of the hills. The water gets shallower and shallower until I feel the bottom of the canoe brush the sand. I get out and start hauling it up towards the shore. The water has been warmed by the sun all day. I wade through it, knee-deep and lukewarm like tea water. I pull the canoe up as far as possible, beaching it up into the sharp-toothed grasses.

After, I can collapse on the sand: rest, drink a little water, eat some honeyed berry cake. The sky's blush has descended into a harsh orange. I watch the sun fall quicker into the horizon. I take a moment to breathe deeply. The wind here is harsh and dry, the air itself so different to the air on our rainforest beaches back home. I close my eyes and relax for a second.

There's a rustling in the grasses. My eyes open, and my throat seizes in a panic. A woman emerges from the dune beside me — she's taller than I am, carrying a net bag in one hand and a sharp stone in the other.

"Ah!" I raise my arms to ward her off, even though I'm still seated on the sand.

She says something, but I can't make it out through the bound and ricochet of unfamiliar hard and soft sounds.

"Nō hea koe? "

She points at me with her knife, at my cedar bark clothes. She is dressed in a skirt made of grasses and not much else. Her hair is knotted on top of her head and coloured a deep red.

"Nō hea koe?" she asks again, sharper this time. "He reo Māori tōu?"

I can only guess what she's asking, and I point towards the island that is far, far back in the direction

I came from. It's already beginning to be cloaked in darkness, but the sun is sitting behind it, the outline of the mountain just visible above the water. I gesture towards my canoe, my paddle on the ground next to me.

She kneels to inspect it, careful not to touch. After a moment she looks up and smiles. She says the name of my village, and I nod.

She sheathes the knife out of sight and throws her bag over her shoulder, then beckons me up. I lift my stuff and stand next to her. She points through the dunes: *Walk forward through the grasses silently.* She looks at me and smiles but doesn't try to talk to me again. Occasionally, as we walk, she points us in new directions. It's getting darker, and soon I can't really see where we're going. The sand turns to damp earth, to mud, and back again. We walk until the moon has risen.

Her village is on top of a hill. We climb for quite some time before the land evens out again. The edges of the village are marked by sharpened fenceposts of hardwood, the tips carved into pointed ends. Here and there are thatched houses made of branches and grasses. Lots of small homes. In the centre of the village is a longhouse made of intricately decorated wood. The cooking fire throws the carvings into relief; the beings carved onto the pillars are made of spirals and beaks. Shimmering eyes of inlay glimmer in the firelight.

People are sitting round the firepit, talking and laughing loudly. The woman who led me here calls out to them over the fence, and silence falls. Figures leave the fire and rearrange themselves in the shadows. Small sounds of argument waft to us. The woman continues calling out, starting a conversation with someone inside the fence. The two voices take turns talking. I am pulled along so we can approach the gate.

I begin to worry about not being able to speak for myself in this new place. I clutch my paddle and satchel tightly, thinking of the beads round my neck.

The call and response continues until we stand in front of the gathered people inside the fence. An older man starts addressing me in the unfamiliar language. He looks directly at me and gestures at the camp, the longhouse, and the bush behind us. I try to look modest, calm, accepting, as the man continues to orate. The woman beside me takes her turn to talk, but when she finishes there's an expectant silence. I realize my inability to speak their language does not exclude me from introducing myself.

So I talk about home, about the mountain and the bays. I mime a flood, a village on the shore, a raven landing on the prow of a canoe. I name my parents and grandparents and great-grandparents and all the names of their villages too. As I speak I unloop the dentalium shells from round my neck and offer them to the man who addressed me earlier. He stoops to accept my gift and nods.

An older woman steps forward and says, "We are glad you have arrived," in my language.

I hear her say the words and can understand her, but from the way she speaks it's clear they're unfamiliar to her mouth. She isn't used to our sounds — which I now understand to be completely different from her own — but she has a fair grasp of words and patterns. She asks after SILE by name. I tell her that it was SILE who sent me here, across the sea.

And then she says, "Āe, I thought she must have. You look like her. Come and sit. Eat and then we'll talk. You have been out on the water all day, nē?"

I follow her to the firepit, where everyone is returning to their seats to eat. Food is being prepared over the open flame, or on top of hot stones. Starchy roots are being pelted with rocks and shaped into cakes. On another fire, smaller and smouldering nearby, someone is cooking what look like the kernels of orange berries. There are fresh greens too, and things from the ocean — fish and clams.

The younger woman beside me produces a decorated gourd and offers it to me. I go to drink but she shakes her head, splashing the water onto my hands instead. It trickles over my fingers and I rinse them. Afterwards she motions for me to flick the water over my body and head.

Then the older woman makes her rounds with the food. She passes me a small bowl. Some bird, some fish, a few vegetables. As I start eating, she names everything in her language — he moa tēnei, he tuna, he kina, he karaka — before explaining what these are in mine. A bird like a giant grouse, some eel, sea urchin, poisonous but delicious berries that must be prepared over several days. The shellfish don't look so different from the ones back home, where SILE leads us in tending the clam beds. Then the woman offers me smaller, sweeter ones, like smooth-shelled clams. I eat until I'm full and can't eat any more, though the women try to get me to taste a few more dishes.

Then we wash again, and the older woman begins her line of questioning.

"Why have you come here?"

"SILE and I watch the ocean often, and for the last week or so we have seen ships move back and forth across the northwest horizon."

"What is so special about them?"

"They're massive and foreign. They move in strange ways. At night many of us have had dreams about those who wait on the ships. They are not like you or us."

I wait for the old woman to say something.

She clears her throat, and thanks me for my message. "We appreciate your care for us, despite all the quarrels of the past. I hope you'll stay for a few days before returning home. You are more than welcome."

"Thank you. I would be very glad to. I barely got to see the island in the sunlight."

"Good. It's settled. You can stay with Whioi in her home." The woman gestures to the one who met me on the beach and led me here. "Whioi is my granddaughter. I am Kui."

"Thank you again." I smile at them both. "I have been wondering how you know SILE and speak our language. Do you speak it here sometimes too?"

Kui laughs. "No, not at all! But I can tell you how it is that I know some of your tongue."

I met her a long time ago, when I was younger than you are now. I'd gone down to the beach to forage. As my view rose over the hill I saw SILE. She was wading through the water towards me. She was towing a small canoe, not unlike the waka we carve here. Even from far away I could tell she was not from this island. Her clothes, the dress she wore — like this.

She fingers the bark dress I am wearing, made of softened and woven cedar.

Her hair too, and her paddle of course. I didn't feel worried when I saw her; I was excited. For a year or two I had been ready to learn what lay beyond this island. It had been so long since we had talked to our cousins across the ocean, and none of our family had any plans to make contact soon. I wondered what had caused the split between our people, and wondered especially if anyone could even remember what had happened.

SILE beached her canoe, and I yelled out to her in greeting. She seemed scared at first, but as I got closer, I smiled and held up my arms in welcoming. I admired the treasures her family had bestowed on her: the hammered metal earrings, the strings of shell beads, the animal leather she wore. Her hair was long and black, and her face looked a bit like mine. But when she smiled her whole face changed; the height of her cheeks pressed into her eyes and created black crescent moons.

As we reached one another I tried to talk to her, but it quickly became clear we didn't share any language. We had to talk like animals do, in gesture and pace and dance. We learned to talk without all the words in the way, sitting in the warm sand and trying to build a language together. Our most important words were the same: horizon, mountain, canoe, woman. Soon she could use her hands to tell me she had been caught in the treacherous currents between our islands. She'd *thought that she might die. She had doubted that she would reach land, let alone find me. I used the length of my arms to tell her there were plenty of people here, over the dunes and through the swamp.*

Before dark I brought her home to the pā, to feed her and let her rest. As she slept, I talked with my mother, who was apprehensive about letting her stay. She was worried about the political implications of hosting her. We came to an agreement that she could stay, but that we would shelter outside the village — in secret. I took food and supplies, and when she woke we travelled to a small hut near the shore that hunters and fishers used when they could not get home before nightfall. We stayed there together for a few days, working in the forest and the sea.

SILE was gifted and could understand ecological relationships with ease. Though the plants and animals here were mostly unfamiliar to her, she could easily guess their importance to one another. She especially loved examining the fish, the tide pools, and the molluscs farther up the coast.

On the last night before she left, we pulled our sleeping mats out and star-gazed. We showed each other how to navigate to our islands and villages. There was discussion about the tides and currents between the islands — tricky to cross and often deadly. SILE was lucky she had made it without guidance.

When dawn came it was time to take her home. I decided to make the trip too, without permission from my mother. We would send word back to the pā that we were staying near the beach for a few more days. I called my pet parrot down from the berry-laden trees. I asked it to take the message back to my mother. The bird listened closely, watching me speak, before bouncing off my arm and back into the trees, its jade band shining in the sun.

And then we were on the sea for a whole day — I had never been on the water so long. It was a very welcome relief when we finally reached the inlet and the beach came into view. It looked more like home than I had expected. Along the beach were smaller trees with knotted red bark. Beyond the sand, trees rose like mountains. They were so tall they blocked out the sun; it made me dizzy to see their trunks reach into the sky. We brought in our canoes and caught our breath. The air was wet with a fine rain, yet the sun was out.

She led me through the forest at the edge of the shore. The birds were shy of me and hid. I heard their tapping on the wood, the echoes of sharp, hard beak on tree. Later, on other walks through these woods, I would find their feathers on the path — very fine, the calamus a bright yellow-orange-red colour that stretched towards the down.

SILE was able to show me her home and name things

in her own language. She used her hands to mime crea-
tures and their actions, and offered warnings about
some of them. Some were so strong and tall and sharp
they left large gashes on the trunks of cedar trees. She
talked loudly and confidently to let the animals know
we were there, but still we stuck closely to one another
on the track.

We reached her village, and I saw a thousand
similarities and differences. Their big house was less
decorated and larger. It was very long and tall, with
welcoming pillars out the front. Everything was carved
from smooth and straight wood. Her family was there,
her whole village. They looked familiar but had fuller
faces than anyone else I knew. They seemed surprised
at her return and embraced her joyfully. There were
bright exclamations in their language; the sounds of
their tongues were thick in click and throat.

We settled in, and later in the evening there were
masked dances. The likenesses of people and animals, in
brightly painted and detailed carvings, danced stories
for us. Parts of the masks moved; beaks opened and
closed with sharp clacks. Some had long hair, some had
blinking eyes. I was terrified and exhilarated.

I spent a few days with her there. Wandering the
forest, she showed me the trails that were barely visible
for the thick moss and ferns. On my final day she took
me up her mountain, the one that sat behind her village.

The trails through the tall cedar forest opened out into rocky meadows. Huge and smooth stones pushed through the lawn of wildflowers. We stopped when the ascent flattened out, in a spot above the sea. The water looked a bright blue from there. The meadow was filled with thousands of brilliantly purple flowers, the colour of which I had never seen before. They were shaped like purple stars, with long stamens in bright yellow. The openness of the meadow was unfamiliar to me; back home the sky opened like this only above the pā, the swamp, the beach, and the sea.

SILE dropped her basket and started praying, burning dried leaves in an abalone shell. The strong smell made my head swirl. Then I watched her grip the stem of a purple flower, pulling up the whole plant with ease. Underneath was a full white bulb. She snapped off the stem and flower and returned them to the ground, stowing the bulb in the basket. She continued until she'd filled the basket in this way.

Later, as we said goodbye to each other, we made plans to meet again. Our moon calendars were already aligned, though our tides were slightly different. About once a month we were able to meet and work together for a few days, helping one another with crafts and chores. We loved each other.

Our parents pretended it wasn't happening; things between our people had not been patched up yet.

Eventually, our parents forbade us from leaving our respective islands. It took a few years, but when it happened, we never saw each other again. I have been tempted many times to visit but was unsure how I would be received. Things haven't been easy for either of us. And now I am too old to make the journey anyway.

I haven't been able to paddle for years now. But I can still see your islands from here, when the weather is smooth and calm. I have never worried about SILE, because I knew she was still across the water, living her own life as wholly as I was trying to live mine. I have missed her for a long time.

Kui turns to me, the lines of age cutting deeper into her skin than before.

I am so happy to see her face again.

I don't know how to reply, tears escaping my eyes.

We stay around the campfires all evening. I feel the tiredness sink deeper into my body. I notice Kui watching as my eyes open and close. There's a hand on my shoulder, and Whioi is dragging me up.

Sleep? she mimes.

"Hmm."

Whioi says her good nights and talks to her grandmother briefly. Then she pulls me towards her house, one of the little thatched buildings nearby. She pushes me inside, passes me my belongings through the door. The hut could maybe sleep three or four, with a hardened dirt floor, which has been smoothed and swept.

"Thank you," I say, wondering how to express gratitude. I move my hands from my chest until they're raised above my head.

We lie down and get comfortable. She says something in her language and rubs my arm, but I'm already falling asleep.

The temperature drops during the night, a cutting chill compounded by rain smattering on the roof. I dream about the howling wind and the sound of wood breaking against rock.

When we wake there's a cool fog over the village. I sit up as Whioi starts moving around the hut, putting the mats away. I watch her apply some of the red earth to her hair, some juice of berries and flowers to her lips. She twists her hair into a knot and secures it with a bone comb with four teeth.

Good morning.

Good morning.

After a full night's rest, I am excited. Kui offered to let me stay, and I have stayed; I've done what SILE asked and now should be free to explore this island as she once did.

Hungry?

Yes, please.

Whioi leads the way out of the house. The village is still quiet, but people are wandering about, completing morning tasks. It seems that some of the noisier men have already gone out to fish. We approach the still hot firepit. I am excited to try more of the food. As we sit down, we're offered two small bowls of what Whioi calls *kai*. A pulpy porridge with berries in it. I eat appreciatively and listen to the fireside chatter. Whioi is very excitable; the news of the ships on the horizon has spread quickly, though no one seems especially worried. Interested but not apprehensive.

I finish my food and try to thank the cooks.

Then Whioi and I stand and take our leave..

We're going to work now, Whioi says. *Back to the beach.*

She gathers her supplies while I try to ask questions.

Where we came from last night?

Yes.

Since we started eating, the children have woken and are tearing through the village with laughs and screams. In daylight I can see the central longhouse is decorated with dozens of detailed figures with spiralling motifs.

Whioi hands me things as she gets ready, including a pair of thin shoes made of reeds. She's already wearing some. I put on mine and adjust the basket she's given me.

What are we doing?

Collecting seaweed on the beach. To dry and eat. For the garden also. Do you do this too?

Yes, often, especially to eat.

Whioi says a quick prayer before we leave. She takes us down the hill through the beginning of the forest. We are quickly plunged into near darkness; even though the morning is bright, the bush is almost as dark as last night. The earth is more fecund here, and there's a familiar dampness, but the air is colder. We follow a trail carved out of hardened earth. Whioi hums as we walk. The birds are singing and talking too, in huge glassy swells and mournful falling notes, but with a permanent chatter underneath.

The walk feels as long as yesterday's. I am less tired but more sore, yet I don't complain. Eventually the hill falls into flatness and the bush dissipates. Suddenly we're in a swamp. The grasses and reeds grow to neck height. They're all the same length, perfectly straight, for as far as I can see. They wave slowly in the wind, small ripples travelling through the homogenous growth. The trail we follow becomes a ridge through the water and mud. The water rises on either side of us. Small fish scatter in puddles. The rushes brush against us. In the distance taller, greener flaxes show their tops — with even taller seed heads.

We use it to make many things. Clothes, rope, baskets.

Important?

Very.

There are plenty of creatures around us. Birds are hungry for bugs and minnows. Shellfish too. Herons wade through the silt with poise. Behind them, clucky waterfowl squabble and hide. We come to the end of the swamp and climb a short but steep hill. Over the other side are dunes, and beyond that is the beach I landed on. My canoe rests where I left it. The sky is a bright azure, last night's wind swept away by the rain, leaving only pillowy and long white clouds that stretch beyond the land.

We'll start here and move down the edge. Whioi points south down the beach.

Sounds good.

I follow her lead, trying to pick and choose seaweed as she does. The lip of the water chases us when we get near, foamy and angry in swells. We try to talk a little as we work, or sing songs. My back quickly aches from the labour. It takes us most of the morning to make our way down the beach.

We stop to wash and eat near a stream that runs

into the ocean. Whioi sits down next to me, and we split some dried meat and fruit. We chew quietly, watching the horizon and listening to the rush of water. I think I can see the tip of my mountain back home, but maybe I'm imagining it.

What are you thinking?

I don't know. Lots of things. Nothing.

How do you feel? Far away from home?

Strange. Okay.

Let's keep working. I want to get home before dusk.

We stand and wash again, lift our baskets, and continue down the beach. The sand turns to pebbles and sharp rocks that have fallen from the land. The water is more violent and the waves crash louder. We turn a bend and find the shore is covered in broken wood, splintered apart by rocks and waves.

Whioi kneels to investigate. I stand beside a group of big stones. Whioi is lifting pieces of wreckage. She heaves up large planks. I go to pick one up from between the rocks. As I pull it up, I see an arm behind the rock, pale and unmoving. My stomach burns and twists. My eyes follow up the hand and wrist into a shoulder and chest. The body it's attached to is almost blue.

Whioi is behind me, pulling me away.

We look at the body, bleached from the sun — fair-haired in clothes worn grey and thin.

DOWRY

a taut skin drum with a padded drumstick to match
a dictionary with the right words in it
the photo of my great-grandmother picking flowers
    in the garden
her hair cropped and cheeks smiling she is little
    more than a shape the light hits
and fades through the reaction of chemicals some-
    one mixed half a century ago
a rich white blanket to wear in winter and a cedar
    hat for the wet seasons
slick lotions and serums made from distillations of
    medicines
that cousin collects when she's home
bracelets and anklets made of dried cherries and
    berries

the deed to Mrs Underwood's house
the second one they built after the first one burned
    down
the sharp eyebrows of the child resting next to her a
    knife
made of stone or metal or bone the tune to the songs
    we were singing
        before
the tune to the song you were singing yesterday
a hole in the skin between my nostrils
stretched with the end of a feather
before inserting a plain ring in its stead
the guitar my grandmother played
a pair of her favourite shoes
a way to say hello how are you doing up there?
a map to all the stars I can't name
a cosmological guide home which never fails
an apology from my father
a way to apologize for my father a DVD copy of
    Smoke Signals
four parallel lines across my cheeks
two or three down the chin
the colour pushed underneath my skin with a needle
    and a nettle fibre
the strands of DNA we lost to smallpox
a set of paints made from ochre

or from animal fat and the charcoaled ends of a
    devil's club stem

a killer fry bread recipe

TAUHOU

Dear Grandmother,

I am writing this song, over and over again, for you.
I am a stranger in this place, he tauhou ahau, re-
introducing myself to your land. After everything,
it is hard not to feel uninvited, but I am small and
take up little space. It must be the way I pick only the
sweetest parts of the fruit to eat first. This is all I eat
before flitting away, which makes me an unappeal-
ing guest. As I grow older, I try harder to finish what
I start, to endure sourness — but it makes me weary
and sore.

Grandmother, I don't mean to pry, but I have so
many things I would like to know. Shall we talk
about your boy? I forgive him, over and over again,
as I write to you. Everything I learn helps me

understand him. I forgive him for myself, and myself only. The permanent injury he caused my mother still softens her body and bends her shoulders down round herself. We are each more hurt and aching than we give one another credit for.

SILE, what is the sky like up there? I remember being told that we all came from the stars, that we were star babies who fell from the sky and into our mothers. We chose to be born when and where we did. I remember being shaken awake at night to climb onto the roof — all of us at once: one man, three women, seven children — to watch star showers rain over the sky. Even now, on my way to sleep, I stop and look up at the stars. Many of them are different here, though I can still make out the planets, satellites, occasional shooting stars.

SILE, please accept these words as gifts and apologies. I have no medicine or food to bring you. Wear my stories as though they are the most beautiful blanket, or a dress, as you'd prefer. Let them carry you through your home and mine, as fine shoes, the kind an old Hollywood starlet would wear.

SILE, how do we explain a hurt and a miss for those we've never met — may never meet? I hope when my body returns to the earth, I will make it up into the stars with you, past the tops of the trees and the cave where Thunderbird lives, over the ocean and all the tiny islands it contains.

TRANSFORMER

When I wake up, everyone has already gone for the day. From the light that slips through the curtain I can tell it's late, and this upsets me because I feel wasteful and lazy. I get out of bed and put on yesterday's clothes. In the mirror a girl passes. She's in the ugly phase of growing out a buzz cut. There are several spots on her head where the hair is missing. It makes her look ugly and sick; it makes me feel shy.

The kitchen has been left in a bit of a mess — half-eaten plates of toast and coffee mugs coated with silt. I have a headache and need a coffee, but both the French presses have been used, and I can't bring myself to wash either. There's an AeroPress in the cupboard I don't know how to use. I turn on the jug and look for a nice slice of bread in the bag, but it's only crusts and stale end pieces, so I settle for a spoonful of peanut butter. I read once that it's important to have protein as soon as you wake up. I drink peppermint tea from the mug I usually keep in my room. The animals are all asleep, and the living room is too hot already, the spring sunlight baking the thick carpets. It smells like lived-in house and faintly of dog.

My phone is dead because I didn't charge it. I look out the window and see the mountain. Even through the thick mesh screen I can make out the tops of the pine trees and the rising peak of the mountain, still barely capped with snow, which appears as static rivulets on the mountainside. Something calls down to me from the top. I suck the peanut butter spoon contemplatively. Outside, the crows are fighting over the garbage cans, the metal lid clattering to the ground. I imagine them jumping around one another in celebration. I cleaned out the fridge last night; there should be enough bounty for them all.

The cat groans and stretches on the couch. She curls back into a ball, a field mouse swaddled in my father's sweater. The radio emits a hum and buzz of conversation and laughter that turns into music. I half tidy the kitchen, to erase my own presence, and leave the rest of the mess for later.

I shower in the small bathroom, where steam pulls paint and wall and laminate away from the bones of the house. It's best to leave the window open. Through it the field out back is a vibrant green — we're halfway through spring, after all — and the thaw has brought the wildflowers to life. The grasses are strong and succulent. Hot water dribbles unsatisfactorily over my body. Cold air wafts through the open window.

Then I dig through piles of laundry in my room, the clean heaps of clothes I don't often wear. Clothes I prefer get washed separately and live on top of the piles. I get dressed and put my shoes on. There isn't much for me to do at the moment. There are stacks of paper that need to be sorted and completed, for school or to find a job. Day to day the importance of each task changes. Today neither feels particularly pertinent, and I don't even pretend to look over or reorganize the papers. The only thing between me and the outside world is tying my shoelaces. I knot loops with care — the laces themselves are fraying, and I know they'll break if I yank them too hard.

The screen door slams behind me on my way out, startling the gang of crows poaching from the trash. I walk out onto the road, which is quieter than usual. I can hear the faint sound of traffic from the highway beyond. The smell of the sea drifts over, but I turn towards the forest and the mountain that sits in the middle. For someone who eats like I do, I feel pretty good on no breakfast. The peppermint tea has settled my stomach and pounding heart. As I walk towards the forest, I make note of who is home and who is not.

Uncle Sam's truck is parked in the driveway, Aunty Betty's van too. It is comfortable to know people are around, even if I can't see them yet.

The road is cracked concrete that turns to gravel closer to the forest. Small pieces catch in the worn sole of my sneaker. I stop to kick out the stone, only for the hole to be filled again as soon as I resume walking. Aunty May's front yard is full of dogs play-fighting. Her son's trailer is to the side of the property, but his truck is gone, so he must be out fishing. The field is the smell of fresh hay and clover.

There at the lip of the forest is a small trail with a gate. I walk through and am enveloped by the coolness. There is a *ki-ki-ki-ki-ki* and a rustling along the ground. I have startled a flicker that's been catching bugs and grubs from the earth. The bird takes off to a branch above my head, bobbing its head along as it watches me. It has a grey spotty body and a red splash that drops below its beak.

"Hello, Flicker," I say. "Sorry for interrupting. I just wanted to go for a walk through the woods today. I feel something calling down from the mountain for me."

The bird looks at me some more, and then says, *Don't worry, friend. I was just about finished eating anyway. Most of the bugs are hiding from the sun now, and I've had my fill, ki-ki-ki. Where are you walking today? Would you like company, ki-ki?*

Flickers are small, unobtrusive birds. This one has a particularly dark-orange head and tail. It twists its delicate head as it waits for my answer.

"If you have the time, I would be grateful for the company."

Wonderful, ki-ki-ki. Are you making your way up the mountain, then?

"Yes. I want to take in the view from the top."

The top, ki-ki-ki. I can go as far as the open wood. Shall we begin, ki?

"Do you mind going this way?" I point towards the main track, which gets the most use by the public.

Wouldn't you prefer to go the old way?

"I only ever stick to this path."

If you're interested, I could show you how I go through the old part of the wood, ki-ki-ki.

So I follow the bird, who hops along the low branches.

Your family is from here, Flicker says.

"Yes. My grandmother's family."

Do you know which crest your family bears?

I shake my head.

That's fine. For today you can be my ward.

We walk in silence for a time, Flicker leading the way through undergrowth that appears to have been undisturbed for some time. I feel guilty for treading on moss and fresh shoots of bush. My footsteps are big and clumsy. Flicker makes only small rustling sounds, the occasional *ki-ki-ki-ki* if they hear something threatening beyond.

Did your grandmother grow up here, ki-ki-ki?

"For a while, before they took her away to one of the schools farther up the island."

One of the bad ones?

"One of the worst. They took all of her siblings, except the youngest. When she came back, she got married and had kids and moved to the city."

The city isn't so far away, ki.

"I think it was at the time, maybe. But my dad came back here eventually. His grandparents raised him here."

Were they kind people?

"I never got to meet them. I hope so. My great-grandfather taught my dad how to work on a boat. He was a fisherman. My great-grandmother was an important aunty to everyone in the village."

Hmph. I wouldn't know them either, ki-ki-ki-ki. I am only a few years old. Maybe my great-great-great-great-grandparents would have known them.

"You seem very wise for such a young bird."

I just listen to my elders, ki-ki-ki. If you pay attention to everyone else around you, you'll learn enough to fill several lifetimes, ki.

"That sounds like something my mother would say."

What kind of woman is your mother?

I don't know how to answer this, so I don't say anything for a while, and then, "She's very resilient."

Resiliency is valuable, ki-ki-ki.

"It is."

Flicker stops on a slightly rotted tree trunk. *A moment please, ki-ki-ki.*

I stand and watch Flicker tap the wood slowly with their hard and straight beak, the sides of which are slightly irregular. Their beak chips and resonates through the wood, and then suddenly they're pecking in a vivid and vibratory blur. In the distance another bird thrums against wood, calling back to Flicker. And then we move on farther through the woods.

"Do you have children?"

Not yet, ki-ki-ki. I was hoping this spring I might have a clutch of eggs to call my own. But no luck.

"I'm sorry about that."

It's fine. I have become more and more afraid of what might happen to them — the creatures that would like to eat them or the summer storms that might blow them away. I have heard others tell me not to worry about that, because otherwise none of us will ever end up having children — ki-ki-ki-ki-ki.

We're hurrying along through the bush now. Flicker seems to be trying harder to lead me through spaces wide enough for my clumsiness to not be so disturbing.

Flicker stops at particular spots and tells me what happened there. Where the bugs are especially good, or where a runaway princess perished a long time ago. The places where, if you look hard enough, you can see the bay through the trees — and if invaders on boats were headed for your village, you would be able to watch them and take note of their numbers, before running back down the hill, homeward.

The incline begins to sharpen, and Flicker says, *I enjoyed this time, friend. Carry on in this way and you should be fine!* before flitting away suddenly, up through the trees and away.

I don't even have a chance to say goodbye or thank you. I'm sad for a moment, and then keep walking, trying to train my eyes to find the path that isn't there anymore. Above, the sky has become a threatening grey, and the air is the delightful wet wash I love so much. I have no idea where I'm going and try not to panic. The sun should be directly above me in the sky, but it's hard to tell behind the cloud. From the treetops small gardens of ferns and other epiphytes fall, gracefully, haphazardly. Swathes of fronds and thick green moss cover tree trunks. A brook sounds faintly nearby, running over craggy stones, keeping the soil nearby moist and fecund. A salamander walks slowly over a bed of moss; someone flaps about in the tree overhead. Twirling down through the air, an orange feather lands at my feet. I pick it up and say thanks, before jumping over the water and carrying on my way.

For some time I have the feeling that someone is there, walking alongside me, but they never stray from the corner of my vision. That's okay — if they would rather not be seen by me, I can accept it. I don't feel threatened, but rather glad for the company after Flicker's abrupt departure.

"How far are you going, friend?" I ask into the silence.

I keep walking and don't expect a reply. Through the underbrush I come across a massive cedar log, completely denuded. I move up to touch it and see what's living inside or on top of it, but find it's a welcome post that has fallen on its side. On the front is a face that's smooth and beautiful, lips curling round the sides of its head in a big smile. It has a body too, and wears a woven cedar hat. I've come to a secluded resting place on the side of the mountain.

The feeling that I'm not alone extends further, blurs the edges of my vision, reaches out to touch the welcome pole. A rush of excitement and joy and sadness bursts in my chest. I stand and look at the pole and wish I knew the proper thing to do, what my ancestors would want me to do. I feel the urge to pray, but I'm not religious. This might be the time my dad would burn some sage or split a cigarette in half, spilling tobacco across the forest floor. But I have nothing, so I just bow my head for a moment.

I don't know whether it's finding the figure lying on the earth or walking so far on an empty stomach, but I begin to feel light-headed. I should have brought water and a snack, but I wasn't thinking that far ahead this morning. It's fine for now. I cast my eye about, in the hope of easy food, but it's too early in the season for most of the berries, so I'll have to go without for now. I sturdy my resolve and move on. The light shifts through the branches and falls in slanted shafts.

There is only the soft blowing of the wind and the shadow in the corner of my eye. It's hard not to fixate on it. The darkness clouds the edge of my vision even more, and I feel the dizzy spell worsen.

"Who's there?" I say. "I'm nothing to worry about." Pain grips my temples, and the wind picks up around me, driving me into a panic. "Who are you?"

And then I'm falling to the ground in black.

A thousand things can happen in a lifetime, and plenty of what happened in mine was unexpected. As a baby my mother drew me to her breast while my father worked his boat. I had brothers and sisters each side of me and was never without company. We played with the dogs along the street while my mother tended her flowers in the back garden. Her hair was a short crop all her life, and I had the same haircut most of the time. We had our problems, but plenty of things were good. We had each other, the fish, the glittering bay that opened out onto the sea.

When they come to take you away, you don't have time to talk to anyone. There is no packing or goodbyes. It doesn't matter if your father is out on the water and won't be back for hours. My mother knew this, and the consequences of failing to give us up, so she decided to do it on her own terms. Each summer she would return us to the school farther up the island, where our hair was cut and we were showered with delousing fluid. She would wave us away, up to the nuns, and we wouldn't see her until the return of the hot sun and berry season.

The school was built of big sneering buildings. The nuns and priests would gather us up in their cold arms and carry us through the gates. Eventually everyone stopped crying, because they enjoyed making us cry. The courtyard filled with silent children. In the night-time the doors to our rooms would open and close, footsteps echoing down the hall. There was the feeling

· 183 ·

of a priest's hand in the bed, the shower, the office. There was a beating, a curse, a sickness. Some of the children were at other schools on floating islands and tried to swim home, only to drown. The graveyard at the edge of the schoolyard grew each year, from outbreaks, starvations, exposures. There was a separate plot for stillborns and girls who died during pregnancy.

When I leave, I'm sixteen. I meet a beautiful man who is all muscle and bravado. He's with the navy but says he'll leave it for me. He wants to marry me too. We have two children first, a girl then a boy, but then I leave him at the altar — so he flees into the night. I manage. Sometimes it's just enough to be gone from that place. My baby brother escapes, the only one of us left untouched by such ungodly machines. I meet another man, we do get married, and we have more children together. A big family like the one I grew up in. But I know what he does to my children, at night or when I'm not home — and I know he doesn't stop at just a hiding, even for the boys.

Some things even a drink can't hide. I know this, but it doesn't make anything easier. Soon I'm the one waving my kids away, as my parents take them from the city back to the reserve. The children return my wave, and then turn to face the front. The younger boy will never mention me to any of his wives or children. The fighting can get worse at any time. My husband likes to make points with his arguments. He says things that make my stomach turn, and the drinks pour themselves faster. The last time we argue, he makes the same threat he's made a thousand times before, only this time he strikes the match.

Me and the girls spend a whole day at the hospital because he doesn't die straight away. Every single part of his body is covered in blistered wound. His screams echo through the ward, and I send the girls away for coffee. When he passes and the doctor comes in with the papers to sign, I finally feel a veil begin to lift. By the time we put him in the ground, it's completely gone. And then it's a few more decades of raising children and grandchildren. It's dinners with my family and playing songs for my nieces, before squirrelling them away into my closet to try on my dresses and shoes — fashionable treasures that delight.

When I die, I don't know how many children there are. I suspect I've met some of them on the sly before, but only briefly. My boy is the kind of man who would bring them to meet me in public and not tell me they're his. He's a snake and a con. He has never forgiven me for any of my actions or inactions. Though he loves women, he hates me. None of them show up to the funeral. It isn't until after — up in the ether — that I can see them all, scattered across both islands. None of them could know, but I see the shape of my face and wave of my hair. When they smile, I see the crinkle of my sister's eyes, the curves of her cheeks and lips. I see all of my granddaughters across the ocean, and it is enough for me. I feel my body burst into stars.

We wake up together on the ground, grandmother and I. Our face is pressed against the firm moss and stones. We're more resolved than ever to make it to the top of the mountain. We move through the forest with purpose; it's easier now, with two of us here. Grandmother says that in the old days everyone would make their way into the forest like this — on their own, without food or supplies. It was your task to find the spirits and guides in the forest. They would appear and bring you gifts and challenges. We are making our way to the top of the mountain in such a fashion. A challenge, a quest.

Together we have double the knowledge of the space around us; our body feels old and young at the same time. There are a thousand new sensations that run around under our skin. I feel everything that happened to her, but there's enough in our heart and body now to soothe it. She never got to do the things that I can now. I feel her try out words in our language, on our tongue, words she may have heard but was never allowed to learn herself. Together in our body we're covered in the marks my friends and I have pulled from outdated anthropological studies. My wrists and ankles and chin are tattooed like women's were a thousand years ago. It feels like we want to weep. But we carry on, through the forest, towards the top.

We both know what's waiting there, in the cave at the top. As we climb, the clouds pool around the peak. The air is frenetic and heady. We're working hard to get there, but it becomes hotter and hotter, tropical lashings of air hitting us. The clouds blacken as we grip the edge of a small cliff and pull ourself up. Above, the sky lowers itself onto our head. We crawl across the lip of the cliff, along and up, until we're crouched at the mouth of the cave.

Inside, the bird is sleeping; black feathers rise and fall as it breathes deep. It's enormous, filling the entire cave. Each feather is easily the length of our arm and glows an otherworldly blue. The air inside the cave is a painful friction. We don't think about what we want or why we're here.

We reach towards the bird, and its eyes open in glaring white light, throwing us outside the cave. We fall on our back against the rock, and the bird flies out of the cave above us. Lightning forks from the sky, and the world flashes black and white. The bird flaps its wings and thunder rolls, breaking the heat, letting rain drop from the sky in pelting sheets.

Why are you here? Thunderbird asks. *Why have you come?*

To see you, we say.

Why? Thunderbird asks again, flapping its black wings, crackling the air blue.

We need to be whole, we say. *Can you please make us whole? Like we were before?*

How do you suppose I do this? Do you think if I could do this, I wouldn't have already done it for you — all of you?

We felt called to this place today, and we believe this is why.

Is it not enough for the two of you to be reunited — united for the first time?

It is. We're very appreciative. We have gratitude, we say.

Quiet, says Thunderbird. *That's enough. I don't take*

*requests. When you wake up, you'll see what XÁLS has
intended for you. That's final.*

With a last burst of lighting, Thunderbird dissipates
in an explosion of hot-aired thunder —

    and we fall from the top of the mountain
    to the earth and sea below
    as drops of rain
    falling in hundreds of thousands
    at once
    flooding the rivers in their valleys
    and lakes in their basins
    we are falling as water
    in divine form
    to wake on the earth
    with the flood receding
    the raven's call
    on the prow of a canoe
    the twist of rope
    on knotted trunk
    we wake
    as infants and clay
    together
    and whole again.

MOTHER

Creator throws them into the ocean, Mother and Daughter, to become islands. This transformation is accompanied by a covenant of mutual care between the people and the new islands.

They lie side by side. Mother wraps herself ever so slightly around Daughter.

A woman is a turtle, a fish, a canoe. A woman is an island. A woman is the only thing between me and drowning.

SENĆOŦEN GLOSSARY

SENĆOŦEN is the language of the W̱SÁNEĆ Peoples, whose traditional territory covers parts of the Saanich Peninsula, the San Juan Islands, the Gulf Islands, and the Georgia Strait. Due to colonization, we now have only five small reserves across some of our old winter village sites. I whakapapa to the W̱SÁNEĆ through my grandmother, Doris Underwood, who was both W̱SÁNEĆ and Snuneymuxw. She was from the SŦÁ,UTW̱ (Tsawout) village. Doris was a residential school survivor and spent much of her life away from the reserve. I have used a small amount of SENĆOŦEN in my writing, in much the same way I have used te reo Māori. I am not fluent in either, but hope to be much more familiar one day. I use these words to bring myself closer to my tūpuna and to spread the fire of our language further. SENĆOŦEN is a critically endangered language that was saved by Matua

Dave Elliott Sr. Through his mahi we have been able to preserve and revitalize the SENĆOŦEN language. The SENĆOŦEN words used in this book have been checked using online sources such as the FirstVoices SENĆOŦEN portal.

ĆENIŦEŁOṈSET	Earth Cooling Down, W̱SÁNEĆ Autumn
ĆENKI,LES	Earth Born Again, W̱SÁNEĆ Spring
ĆENŦOŁEṈ	Cold Earth, W̱SÁNEĆ Winter
ĆENQÁLES	Hot Earth, W̱SÁNEĆ Summer
HÍ,ÁȻE	Goodbye
MÁN	Father
SÁĆS	Aunt / Uncle
SILE	Grandmother / Grandfather
SḴEKĆES	Red Huckleberry
SṈITȻEŁ	"Tod Inlet," the first W̱SÁNEĆ village site
SX̱IMÁŁEŁ	Esquimalt, a suburb of Victoria, Vancouver Island

TÁN	Mother
WEXES	Spring peeper frog
XÁLS	Creator

TE REO MĀORI GLOSSARY

This Māori language glossary was compiled from two main sources. The first was my own very limited reo (language), which I used while writing and checked using Te Aka, the online Māori dictionary: maoridictionary.co.nz. The definitions of the words below are the meanings that I have learned and used in my own life. As such, they are casual and may differ from other translations. They are in no way "official" or "correct"; they are my living, modern understandings of Māori words and ideas. This is also why I used an online resource to check and clarify my translations.

āe	to agree, yes
Aotearoa	land of the long white cloud (New Zealand)
hākari	to feast, banquet

hāngi	earth oven
hapū	to be pregnant / kinship group, subtribe
kākahu	to dress, cloak, apparel
kare	friend, dear
korowai	cloak ornamented with pokinikini
kuia	older woman (aunty, grandmother, elder)
Kurawaka	beach where the first woman was formed
Maunganuioteao	river that runs through the Erua forest
moko	tattoo / grandchild
muka	soft inside of beaten flax, used for fine weaving
pā	fortified village
Pākehā	settlers in Aotearoa of European descent
paru	to be dirty / dirt, mud, earth
piupiu	to wave about / garment made of flax

pokinikini	curled strips of flax
pou	post, pillar
taiaha	long wooden weapon
taniwha	water spirit / powerful leader
taonga	treasure, valuable objects, resources, ideas
tēnei	this, here
te reo Māori	the language of Māori
Te Tiriti	the Māori version of the Treaty of Waitangi
tupuna (singular); tūpuna (plural)	ancestor(s) (West Coast dialect)
urupā	burial ground, cemetery
waiata	to sing / song, chant
Waikawa	a bay / settlement near Waitohi (Picton)
waka	canoe, vehicle
whaea	mother / aunt / aunty
whakapapa	to recite in proper order / genealogy
wharekai	kitchen, dining hall

Plants and Animals

horopito	pepper tree, native bush
kākāpō	a rare, endemic ground parrot
kanuka	white tea tree (similar to manuka)
karaka	native tree with large, orange berries
kawakawa	ceremonial shrub with heart-shaped leaves
kereru	wood pigeon
kina	common sea urchin
kiokio	drooping ground fern, found near streams
mamaku	black tree fern
manuka	tea tree
ngaio	native tree with white timber
pūkeko	purple swamp hen
ruru	native owl
tarata	lemonwood with fragrant flowers and gum

tauhou	silver eye / stranger / newcomer / novice
tī kōuka	cabbage tree
totara	very large native conifer
tuna	freshwater eel

Phrases

e kare	my friend
E pēhea ana koe?	How are you?
He kai kei aku ringa	There is food at the end of my hands (proverb)
he tauhou ahau	I am a stranger / silver eye bird
Kia ora, whaea	Hello, Aunty

AUTHOR'S NOTE

This book has been inspired by many things, including my Māori and W̱SÁNEĆ whakapapa. This writing is entirely imagined and doesn't reflect any real iwi or culture. It uses parts of my own whakapapa, but only very broadly. This work cannot and should not be used to educate oneself about either of these cultures. It is purely fictional and blends many places and stories together. It is not supposed to be an accurate, traditional, or "correct" perspective on any Māori or Coast Salish people or culture. I have purposely pushed the two sides of my whakapapa together to reflect my own experience, not the reality of the Indigenous people of Aotearoa and Turtle Island.

The only things that are completely and unequivocally true in this work are the effects of colonization and genocide against Indigenous people, such as pollution, land neglect and abuse, domestic violence, the legacy of residential schools, urbanization, cultural and familial disenfranchisement, children in state care, suicide, and mental and physical illness. I have described only part of my experience with these things, and just a tiny fraction of what Indigenous people experience across all the oceans.

ACKNOWLEDGEMENTS

Thanks to my MA class (IIML '20) and the IIML staff, especially Emily Perkins and Anahera Gildea. Alison Whitakker for her encouraging early reader's report. Joy and Linda for their patience and love. Fergus and the whole THWUP team for backing me. Tayi Tibble for her amazing feedback and promotion of this mahi, as well as the initial inspo to be a young Māori wahine writer! Shirarose for reading this manuscript and truly seeing it — it meant everything to me. The House of Anansi Press team for all their support and excitement. Ebony Lamb for the unbelievable author photos. Thank you to the Adam Foundation, Newsroom, and Dick Frizzell for the financial support that helped me finish this book. HÍSWKE to the NDN cousins I found on the internet who inspire my writing, most notably PEPAKIYE. Thanks to all of my family: Robyn and Brian, the whole extended Patchett whānau. Margi and

Rob for welcoming me into your life and taking such amazing care of me. My wife, Olive, for everything. Momoka and Parsley Nuttall, who keep me tethered to this mortal plane. My parents, Tina and Lorry, for being great parents, mentors, and my best friends. Extra thanks to Lawrence for his editing work on this manuscript. To my baby sister Aquila, these stories are yours too. All the ancestors, especially the tūpuna wāhine who helped me write this book: Makereti, Mata, Titihuia, Catherine, Hazel, and Doris — who started everything.

The whakataukī (proverb) that appears in the epigraph of this book is discussed in sources that include: Leonie Pihama, Hineitimoana Greensill, Hōri Manuirirangi, and Naomi Simmonds, *He Kare-ā-roto: A Selection of Whakataukī Related to Māori Emotions* (Hamilton: Te Kotahi Research Institute, 2019), and Hirini Moko Mead and Neil Grove, *Ngā Pepeha a Ngā Tīpuna: The Sayings of the Ancestors* (Wellington, Victoria University Press, 2001).

© Ebony Lamb

ĸŌTUKU TITIHUIA NUTTALL (Te Ātiawa, Ngāti Tūwharetoa, W̱SÁNEĆ) holds an MA from the International Institute of Modern Letters. She won the 2020 Adam Foundation Prize and was runner-up in the 2021 Surrey Hotel-Newsroom writer's residency award. She lives on the Kāpiti Coast of Aotearoa New Zealand.